Fictional Musings

A Collection of Short Stories and Poems

BRITTANY L. ADKINS

ISBN: 978-1-7321453-3-7

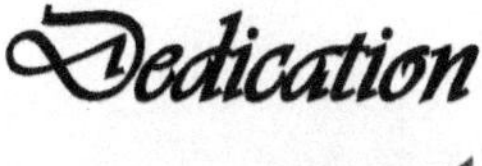

To my husband and children, thank you for the support and love.

Dedication

To my husband and children, thank you for the support and love.

Letter to my readers:

Thank you so much for reading my book! You make this dream possible! These stories and poems are a showcase of some of the various genres I like to write in. You reading this book means the world to me, and I hope you enjoy it!

I should warn you that some things within these pages may be triggering for some, so please read with care.

Trigger warnings:

Cancer, death, polyamory, sex, MFF relationships, anxiety, ableism, demons, gore, occult, pregnancy, monster sex, age gap, attempted murder, blood, sexually explicit scenes, sexual harassment, there may be more, but these are the big ones.

Check the author's website if you want to see the full list.

Tropes:

Friends to lovers, oblivious to love, pen pals, love triangle, star-crossed lovers, age gap, all grown up, beauty and the beast, protector, afraid to commit, military romance, instalove, spontaneous.

All my best,

Contents

Acknowledgments

Thank you to my best friend, James, for cheering me on!

Thank you to my editor, Kala Fleming-Crowe.

The Day I Should Have Died

Remorse…regret…love…joy…peace. These are the emotions coursing through me as I sit here on the deck of my cabin, watching the sun come up through the fir and cedar trees surrounding the cabin. I never thought I would be here. It doesn't feel like it's been a year, not with the year I have endured. Here I sit, reflecting on how I should have died today.

As the cool breeze brushes against my skin, I pull my Navajo blanket tighter around me and take a sip of my coffee. The birds sing as the morning light welcomes them. Their melodies bring back a flood of memories from this transformation.

It's amusing when you go to the doctor; you never envision you would be the one called into an office versus the exam room. It's odd how this all started with fatigue and a headache that refused to go away. Test after test, appointment after appointment, my life appeared devoured by them until my doctor called and said they had some findings to discuss. The office was quiet but well-adorned with fine art and pretty tropical plants. I figure they were attempting to make it feel welcoming instead of alarming.

Sitting here waiting for the doctor is torturous. *Why do they always make you wait? As if my blood pressure isn't already a little high, I am sure it's even higher now.* You lose all sense of direction in your mind wondering what could be wrong: a malignant tumor, an aneurysm, or something more awful. What could be worse than those? The door opened, making me jump out of my fearful thoughts. I constrained a grin for my doctor.

She grinned at me as she sat down. "Sorry to keep you waiting, Halee. Thanks for coming in. I know the last few months have been terrible with all the tests, but we wanted to ensure we had all the answers we could get." She said, tucking a piece of her blonde curly hair behind her ear. She looked at me with a concerned expression plastered all over her ivory face, but the blue eyes told the truth. They were screaming, "I'm sorry."

I nodded and forced a grin to shroud my fear. "It's all right. I am glad you were thorough. So, give it to me straight, no chaser." I said, trying to sound brave even though my smile was gone.

She opened the file and nodded. "Halee, I am sorry, but

you have stage four metastatic lymphoma. There are treatment options, but it has spread from your lymph nodes to the brain, lungs, and liver. We can aggressively fight this…."

Somehow after she said stage four, my ears no longer heard her. My brain only heard the twisted sound of time ceasing. I was dying. I wanted to cry, scream and punch her in the face, but none of it would have been any use. The most frightening part of all was I was only thirty-one years old, and I was dying.

She walked to the front of her desk, sat beside me, and took my hand. "Halee? Halee?" She called, seeing my face.

"H-h-how...how long?" I stammered, looking at her with a dazed expression.

I needed to know how long to tell everyone. In the midst of my processing, I was suddenly confused because my face felt wet, and I didn't understand why. I reached up and wiped my face. Looking at my hand, it was wet with my tears. I was so stunned that I didn't even realize I was crying.

"Six months, perhaps a year at most, if we do nothing, but we can fight it. Though I must tell you, even fighting it could still be that long. If you do nothing, it could even be less. These cancers are aggressive and hard to catch until they have spread. We can still fight, and some win." She replied, trying to sound hopeful.

"What are my odds?" I asked, sobering up to the news.

"About ten percent. It sounds impossible, but that percentage was three percent five years ago. The more we learn about cancer, especially these types, the more we know how to fight them and win. You could be the one that brings it to eleven percent. You have to have hope," she said, still holding my hand, trying to comfort me.

I stared blankly at her for what seemed like a thousand years, but suddenly a smile crept across my face as I began to laugh. The laugh was soft at first but grew louder and more hysterical. Everything she told me felt like a joke, and I was the butt of it.

Still chuckling, I knew I needed to leave. I couldn't take any more. "I am sorry. I uh...I need to go...I will call you." I told her as I stood up, grabbed my purse, and headed for the door.

"Halee, we need to schedule treatment now. You don't have much time. See my nurse on the way out. Please?" she said, genuinely worried.

"Yeah, okay," I said, leaving before she could say anything else to me.

I couldn't take anymore, I had to get out of there, but something made me stop and see her. Amy was Dr. Singer's nurse. We had become friends during all the appointments. I walked up to her desk drudgingly.

She looked up at me with concern in her bright green eyes. She stood, then walked around the desk and hugged me tightly. I couldn't tell you why my hands tangled in her soft, straight, long raven hair as I buried my face against her neck and sobbed silently into her royal blue scrubs.

She softly stroked my hair and whispered, "It will be okay," repeatedly. Her arms held me close to her as my body shuddered with each horrible sob.

As my tears began to subside, she wiped them away gently and gave me a soft, reassuring smile, which I had grown to love. She returned to her desk and quietly helped me schedule my first treatment.

She stood, returning to my side as she handed me the appointment card. "I will be there to hold your hand as often as I can, I promise," she said to me, then walked out with me to my car.

I was sure she was breaking a lot of rules for me, but she didn't care, nor did I. When we reached my car, she hugged me again tightly. There was silence between us, but we knew what needed to be said to each other. She kissed my cheek and headed back inside as I got in my car and drove home.

Later that night, my boyfriend Cal, my sister Julie, and my parents arrived at my house at 7:30. I know I should have called, but I needed time to pull myself together, and that was something I couldn't do with them all freaking out on the phone. So, texting them was the only solution. I let everyone in and sat with them in the living room.

Cal was ex-military, so his strong frame and stoic look were expected, but you could see in his eyes he was worried. I could tell my mother had just gotten a haircut that day because she wouldn't stop fidgeting with how short it was. She dyed it so no one would notice greying roots with each passing year. She and I look so much alike. I was sad to think I wouldn't see her age. My father was a quiet man and always had been. His country, Irish roots had taught him to listen more than you speak and work harder than you played. He looked at me nervously, massaging his calloused hands. My sister Julie was a mother of four and three years older than me. She and her husband were the types of people that everyone hoped to become. She tucked some of her long red hair, like mine, behind her ear as she texted her husband.

I gave them all a gentle smile, this was the quiet before the storm, and I was the one bringing it down on them.

I took a deep breath and looked down at my shaking hands.

"Darlin', what is it? It can't be that bad. You aren't pregnant, are you?" My father asked with a nervous smile.

Cal looked at me, wondering now if that was true. "Are you?" he asked, trying as hope and excitement filled his eyes.

I shook my head with a sarcastic chuckle. "No. I wish I were…." I paused for a moment seeing my words dash their hopes. "As you all know, I haven't been feeling well for a while. I went to the doctor, and they ran a lot of tests…" I began but pausing, trying to hold back my emotions and tears. The lump in my throat made it hard to talk and fight the emotions. I wanted to swallow it back, but it wouldn't leave me.

Looking up at them, I could see my family practically holding their breath, with fear filling their eyes. Here comes the storm.

"They finally had some answers for me…" I continued before Cal interrupted me.

"Babe, just tell us. You are freaking us out," he said, trying to sound reassuring, but I knew the tone when he was scared.

I took another deep breath. "I have stage four metastatic lymphoma. It has spread pretty much everywhere..." I told him before my mom interrupted me.

"No, you don't! You can't! You are my daughter! These things don't happen to us. They just don't!" she said, standing up, scolding me like I had done something horrible.

I knew she was in shock and denial. Hell, I was there a few hours ago. But I couldn't stop the tears now flooding my eyes.

"I do, Mama. It does happen. 'Cause I have it," I said as

the dam broke and tears rolled down my cheeks.

"No…you can't…" She continued to deny it, but tears now flooded her eyes too.

"How long?" Cal asked stoically.

"A year, at most. If I fight it, I could still only live that long." I said, wiping tears from my cheeks.

"If? You will fight, right?" Cal asked, fighting his emotions.

"Yes, of course. My first treatment is Friday."

I watched my father begin to cry as my sister sobbed against his shoulder.

My mother's knees seemed to give out as she collapsed to the floor in front of my father. "Tell me this is a nightmare?" She asked my father. "How dare you take my daughter from me…" She cursed upward as if she had the direct line to God's ear.

My father grasped her shirt and pulled her up to him.

The chaotic storm erupted in the room, all shouting, crying, and trying to process all the news I had just laid on them. It seemed as if time had stopped again for me. It felt like I was watching all this through a window, but I was not there. It was a feeling that was not only overwhelming but also heartbreaking.

Cal was the most silent of them all. Tears slowly streamed down his face as if he had witnessed the horrors of war again.

It wasn't long before he stood up and told me he had to go because he couldn't take it, and with a quick kiss on the cheek, he was gone. The military had prepared him for many things, but nothing like this. My mother and sister sobbed as my dad silently cried, holding them both. Watching them, it was as if I had already died, but the truth was I had died a little that day.

The day of my first treatment had arrived. I looked at myself in the mirror as I got ready. My eyes were swollen and still blood-shot from crying myself to sleep.

I had thought I would have heard from Cal or anyone the last few days, but my world was silent. *So much for the support,* I thought to myself as I turned on the shower.

As I was about to undress, I heard my front door open and close. Only one person besides my landlord had a key, Cal. I walked out and saw him standing in the living room.

"What are you doing here?" I asked him curiously.

"I am sorry, I needed a few days. Not easy to deal with when the woman you love tells you she has cancer, but I am here now. I will be here for you through this." He said with a gentle smile.

Tears flowed from my eyes as I rushed over and hugged him tightly. I sobbed against his stone-like chest.

He held me close and let me cry. I could feel his lips placing soft kisses on the top of my head.

When the tears finally let up, he smiled down at me. "What can I do to make today better?" he asked me, wiping my tears away.

"You are already doing so much. I am scared and stressed about it. The paperwork the doctor sent me terrifies me," I replied, still sniffling.

"Well, let's start the day with a smile. Come on." He said as he led me to the bathroom.

He saw the shower was running, pulled his shirt over his head, tossed it on the floor, and undid his belt as he kicked off his boots.

I watched him, confused. "What are you doing?"

"Improving your morning. We have a while until your appointment. It is at ten, or did I get the time wrong?" he said, pushing his pants and boxers down.

I looked over that sexy body of his and smirked, shaking my head. "No, that is right."

"I want to hold you and make you feel safe before we have to leave," he said, moving to me and slowing pulling off my sweatshirt.

My eyes met his as I slowly pushed my yoga pants to the floor. Surprise filled me when he took my hand and helped me into the shower.

His arms slipped around me from behind as he held me under the warm cascading water. After a moment, I felt his lips softly kissing my shoulder and neck as his hands began to wander.

Usually, I would have scolded him for trying to ruin the moment by being a horn ball, but this time, I welcomed it. I wanted to feel like I wasn't sick or being stalked by death.

I guided his hands on my body—one to my breasts and the other to my soft mound.

I felt his kisses stop as he whispered in my ear. "Are you sure? It's okay if you aren't up for it."

Nodding, I pushed his fingers between my folds. "I want it. I may not feel like it after the treatments. So, make love to me while we still can."

He kissed my neck and began to rub my clit slowly. His strong fingers were seductively gentle, and they knew each spot to make me melt into his arms. It wasn't long before his erection pressed between the cheeks of my ass, begging to be inside me.

I turned around to face him, and his lips found mine quickly. He pushed me against the shower wall as my tongue found his. I lifted my leg and wrapped it around him. It was the only invitation he needed as he thrust deep into me. His free hand grasped my standing thigh and pulled it up around him. He held me against him effortlessly.

My moans of pleasure echoed into the kiss as he pulsed in and out of me. His hands held my thighs firmly as he pulled me to meet his thrusts. Each thrust buried deep inside me.

Cal knew how to make love. Every time he never failed to make me feel like the most desired woman. It was one of the many things I loved about him.

He broke the kiss and reunited his lips with my neck as he picked up the pace.

My legs locked around him as he drove me closer to my release.

He groaned against my neck. "I am getting close, baby. Where do you want it? Or would it matter if I…"

"Came inside? I doubt it. Fill me up." I told him, panting in lustful pleasure.

A few quick, hard thrusts were all it took to make me cry out in pleasure as I orgasmed. It was the invitation Cal needed to release.

I kissed him passionately as I felt him finish, filling me.

I would have begged for another round if I had known that was the last time, we would make love for many months.

In the coming months, Cal moved in to help me with the coming storm of appointments, treatments, and the chaos of side effects that would follow. Initially, it was a nice gesture, but in the end, it would become a plaguing curse upon our relationship.

I had grown very weak from the treatments, and Cal had done something I never expected him to do, use his trust fund from his father he never spoke to, so he could take care of me.

He looked over the paperwork he had gotten from the doctor. "I think I will try to make you some of these recipes and see if we can't get your strength back up."

"Those sound horrible. I don't eat kale or any of that crap. You knew the chemo would make me nauseous and make it difficult to eat. Why don't you put all that down and come snuggle with me? We can even watch an action movie. Please?" I asked him softly. It was too hard to talk much louder.

"Yeah, sure, later, okay? I am going to the store. Do you want anything? I need to get your prescriptions too," he said at me rather than to me.

"Sure, a bottle of pinot," I said sarcastically.

"What? Halee, you can't drink on your meds. You know that. I will be back later. Love you," he said, grabbing his jacket and walking out.

"Yeah. I know." I said as my phone chimed.

I picked up, seeing the text from Amy. "How are you feeling?"

"Not great. Pretty weak, and Cal isn't helping."

A moment later, my phone chimed again with her response. "What is he doing?"

I sighed as I thought about how to explain it. "He is more on top of my treatments than I am. He drives me to every appointment and talks to the doctors as if he could save me all by himself. I feel like each appointment is taking us further and further apart. Being so distant from him is so hard right now. Some days I feel closer to you than him. You are there for me when he is too focused on everything to see me."

"Cal is trying in his way. I can see how much he loves you. Just be patient with him. Want me to come over? We can lay in your bed and watch chick flicks. I will bring junk food if you want."

I tried not to cry, thinking about how amazing she was to me. "Tea and crackers. It's all I can keep down right now. The chemo is making me too queasy to keep things down."

I waited impatiently for the next chime, feeling like forever before it finally came through. "On my way."

A few nights later, my hair began to fall out from the chemotherapy, and I was angry. I was angry at my body, my mom and dad who were so distant, and my sister, who always cried when she saw me, but most of all, I was angry at Cal. He had always been my rock, but now he was a vast ocean that I was drowning in.

As he entered the bathroom and saw my beautiful, long red hair in clumps in the sink, he met my tear-filled eyes with silence and shock, as if it wasn't real for him until then.

"Aren't you going to say something? Anything?" I yelled at him, scared and furious.

He just looked at me, so scared and shaking, before he finally spoke. "Y-y-you're dying…" he said barely above a broken whisper.

"Yes! I am fucking dying! Where are you?! You are so

wrapped up in my cancer that you haven't even realized I am losing this battle in front of your eyes!" I screamed at him, now shaking.

"I-I-I'm sorry…" he began, before he turned and left the bathroom.

I was sure maybe he needed a moment to pull it together, but then I heard the jingle of his keys and the front door to our apartment open and close. He left. I stood there stunned momentarily before looking at myself in the mirror. He left, and now I had been betrayed by the man I thought I loved and my body. I screamed in anger and threw my hairbrush into the mirror, shattering it. I pulled at my hair, trying to rip it from my head, before the dizziness caught up with me, making me collapse to the ground. I fell over onto the rug and cried for what seemed like hours as I died a little more that night.

Hours later, I woke up and saw he still hadn't returned. I put on a hoodie and pulled the hood up. I texted Amy and told her I needed her. The pain had gotten so bad it was hard to move without wanting to cry, and as much as I hated it, I needed something to take the edge off. I grabbed one of the joints that Cal had rolled for me and the lighter and walked slowly outside, hoping not to fall. When I closed the door, I saw him sitting on the tailgate of his truck in the driveway.

"I thought you had left," I said softly, startling him.

He didn't look up at me. He just stared at his hands as if somehow they were the answer to all of our problems. I wanted to take his pain.

"Sorry, I didn't mean to scare you," I explained, walking over and sitting beside him.

I could see he had been crying. It was hard to watch my big tough military man cry. I tried to take his hand, but he wouldn't let me touch him.

"Cal, I need you. I can't do this without you." I tried to explain to him, shivering in the cool night air of early fall.

He shrugged off his leather jacket and put it around me. "Halee… I don't know if I can be the strength you need. I am trying to, baby. I am. But you were right tonight. I should have been here for you when I wasn't. I don't know how to anymore." He took the joint out of my hand and lit it up before taking a hit and handing it to me.

"Are you breaking up with me?" I asked, shocked, taking the joint back.

At that moment, I realized we weren't cursed, only terrified of losing each other. "God, no! I love you, and always will. I want to grow old with you… I am just scared I won't get to, and I am unsure what to do," he said as Amy pulled into our driveway.

"I thought you were gone. I needed help. Just be here for me and remind me that you love me." I said, kissing him softly on the cheek before taking a hit from the joint.

"You, okay? You shouldn't be out here without a blanket. I will go grab one." Amy told me, running into the house.

"I am going to bed. I will sleep on the couch so you girls can have the bed and have a slumber party. Love you," he said, kissing me tenderly before heading to the house.

I took another hit off the joint. "I hate this shit. He is freaking out. I feel like hell, and now I am smoking weed in my driveway. What a crazy turn my life has taken." I told Amy, almost in tears.

"Hey…it's just a few more treatments, then we will see how you are doing. He is doing his best, just like you. I see cancer patients every day at work. So, I have a leg up on this compared to him." She reassured me by tucking a piece of hair behind my ear, but it fell out in her hand.

She looked at me sadly before opening her car's back driver-side door to get something out of her back seat. "I knew this day might come, so I had a 'bald is beautiful emergency kit' made. We used to give them to our patients when the chemo made their hair fall out. Finish that joint, and we will make you even more beautiful," she said, holding a canvas bag full of stuff.

I took a long final hit, put the joint out, and walked inside with her. I looked up seeing Cal on the couch reading a Michael Connelly novel. He looked up and gave me a soft smile as we passed him.

We walked into the bathroom. Amy began rooting around in the bag. "Hey, Cal, could you bring me a chair from the dining room?"

A few minutes later, he walked in carrying the chair. "What are you two up to?"

Amy smiled and took the chair. "I'm shaving her head. Unless you want to?" she said, offering him the clippers as I sat down.

"Nah, you will make it even. I would miss spots," he said, trying to make a joke, but we both could hear the sadness in his voice.

I looked over at him as he leaned against the door frame and watched Amy turn the clippers on.

"Ready?" Amy asked, meeting my eyes in the mirror.

"I guess so," I replied, closing my eyes.

I couldn't watch. It was hard enough to look at myself in the mirror anymore, but watching this made me scream on the inside. I gripped my yoga pants with a death grip as I felt her pull my long hair back so she could start shaving.

I let out a whimper as I fought my terror and the anger

inside me as I heard the buzz of the cutting hair. I felt someone grab my hands and hold them tight.

I opened my eyes to see Cal kneeling in front of me. His strong hands held mine firmly, letting me know it would be okay.

"Squeeze hard as you can if you need to, baby. I can take it," he said as his blue eyes connected with my green eyes.

I squeezed tighter as I let out a sob. Amy stopped momentarily, letting me cry and have my moment with Cal. He was my rock again.

After a few minutes, she turned the clippers on as my sobs subsided and continued. I could see the locks of my hair falling all around me on the floor as she shaved it all off.

When she finished, she put the clippers on the counter and brushed the bits of hair off my shoulders and neck before handing me a mirror. "You should shower," she said softly.

I looked at my once beautiful self, now sitting bald in the chair. It wasn't horrible, but it was hard to see myself without hair. I set the mirror down and started to stand, but my legs gave out. Cal caught me and pulled me into his arms.

"I got you. Come on, I will help you," Cal said softly, as he helped me stand and undress.

Amy watched for a moment, then started out of the bathroom. "I will just be out here when you get done." She met Cal's eyes.

Cal looked at me and looked back at Amy. "Why don't you join us?"

Surprise graced my face. "Are you sure?" I asked him.

"If we all want that," he said, pulling off his shirt.

Amy walked back in and closed the door. "Okay."

At that moment, we all realized we needed each other to

continue forward down this road.

For the next few weeks, Amy stayed with us. We talked, laughed, and grew closer than we had already become. The odd thing was, I was falling in love with her and deeper in love with Cal.

That following Monday, Cal helped me tie the beautiful scarf covered in red lilies around my head. Amy packed the bag of things I could need. It would be a long day for all of us.

Cal walked me out to his crew-cab truck and picked me up, putting me in the passenger front seat. He then took the blanket from Amy and put it on my lap.

Amy got in the back seat and squeezed my shoulder softly. "We will be there for you all day," she reassured me.

"I know. I just hate these scans. Then I have a treatment after them. It makes it a hard day. I would lose it if it weren't for you two," I replied as Cal got in the driver's seat.

"Lose what?" he asked, missing the first part of my reply.

"My sanity. I was telling Amy about how I am not looking forward to today."

"Well, that's why we will be there," he said with a smile, a genuine smile. It was one of the first since we left the apartment.

He took my hand as he began to drive to the hospital.

I laid on the chemo-reclined chair four hours later, trying to sleep. Sleeping through the mild burning of the liquid pouring into my veins was hard.

"We haven't talked about it, but do you both want to keep whatever we are doing?" I heard Amy softly ask Cal.

"At first, no. Now? Yes. Amy, I can't explain what happened in the last couple of weeks. It's like I woke up grateful for you and falling for you, and I was already so in love with her. It was like being home after searching forever for it. I know she loves you. You were the piece of our lives that was missing," Cal replied to her quietly.

The truth left his lips as if it were the gospel of our lives. It was like Amy was the final missing piece to our puzzle. We were home.

I felt Amy's dainty hand take mine. "I have loved her for years, and until that night, I had never thought of even belonging to a man, but it was everything I needed. I just wish this wasn't under these circumstances."

"Well, then stay, and we will be a family," I said softly with my eyes still closed but smiling.

Two weeks later, Dr. Singer called me in to tell me the update on my latest scans. Amy no longer worked for her because she enjoyed working part-time in the hospital and spending time with us. We sat in her office, trying to stay calm as we talked quietly. Dr. Singer finally joined us and looked surprised to see Amy sitting with me, holding my hand, and Cal standing behind me with his hands on my shoulders.

"Halee, it's good to see you, and I have good news for once." Dr. Singer said as she sat down and smiled excitedly at us.

"Please, Dr. Singer, don't keep me waiting. I don't have much time left," I said with a soft smile, knowing I only had two months left of my year.

"Your treatments worked. Your tumors are shrinking and disappearing. You beat the odds!" she said excitedly.

I turned to Amy, cupped her face in my hands, smiled, and kissed her. The kiss was soft and sweet at first but soon deepened to the level of intimacy we both had come to share.

I then turned and kissed Cal with the same intimacy and passion. With them, I felt like I was home and safe from the cruelties of my cancer and the haunting feeling of death. It was with them both; I found my soulmates. That day we left hand in hand, finally giving into what was there all along.

A month later, Cal, Amy, and I had bought a cabin with a small tract of land in the mountains, about thirty minutes from the city. My family was elated that I was going to live but heartbroken that I was now with Amy and Cal. My family thought I was stupid for moving to the mountains with Amy and him.

I wasn't stupid. A brush with death causes changes in a way that is indescribable to people who have never faced it. Like the phoenix reborn from the grave of ashes, we return anew and grow from our little brushes with death. Life is always with us, but so is death—every moment of our lives.

The memories are still as fresh as yesterday in my mind.

Though some are still as painful as an old wound that still aches when it rains, others bring a smile to my face. Like now, as I see my beautiful girlfriend come out to join me on the deck, the recollection of the memories is still fresh in my mind, making a smile drift across my face.

She kissed me tenderly as she sat next to me. “How are you feeling today?” Amy asked, sipping her coffee as she looked at me.

“Good, but mixed emotions,” I replied.

“That is to be expected…I am happy you are still here,” she said, squeezing my hand.

“Me too.”

“So am I,” Cal replied, kissing my neck softly before taking a seat on my other side.

Every time I died this year, I was reborn into someone stronger, more in love with life and the person I have become. It is interesting to think the day you die may be the day you live instead.

Consuming Darkness
A BATTLE WITH MULTIPLE SCLEROSIS

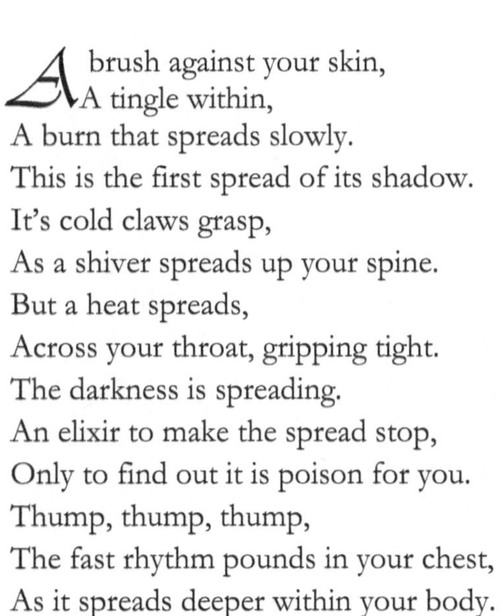

A brush against your skin,
A tingle within,
A burn that spreads slowly.
This is the first spread of its shadow.
It's cold claws grasp,
As a shiver spreads up your spine.
But a heat spreads,
Across your throat, gripping tight.
The darkness is spreading.
An elixir to make the spread stop,
Only to find out it is poison for you.
Thump, thump, thump,
The fast rhythm pounds in your chest,
As it spreads deeper within your body.

Your mind feels dark under its heavy clutch.
Your words are no longer yours.
Your memories are no longer yours.
The darkness consumes more of you.
Down your spine, it drips and flows,
Like blood seeping out of a jagged wound.
Each drop brings a searing pain,
A pain that will never end.
You scream and cry, hoping to fight,
But your only escape is ignorance.
Ignore the pain.
Ignore the memories you have lost.
Ignore the cold and the burning.
Ignore it all.
Each day that passes is a roulette of fear.
Today it has spread more.
The sensation of touch is fading,
Glimmering away like a mirage.
Clench your fists and fight a little more,
But you know it's no use.
Darkness doesn't laugh at your fight,
It stays silent as death.
It only can consume.
Tomorrow when you wake, you may feel normal
Is the darkness gone, or is this too a mirage?
It is the monster that lives within
It's never gone, but only silent,
Planning its next move.
The only question that remains is,
What will it consume in you next?

Meeting My Soldier

I dressed casually in a black college tee shirt from the University of Texas, my favorite dark blue jeans, and my black 'chucks.' I didn't realize this wouldn't be a casual event at the time. I looked in the mirror at my slender waist and well-formed breasts and sighed, realizing it was as good as casual would get. Part of me wished I was prettier, but I knew he wouldn't have wanted to meet me if I wasn't pretty to him. I grabbed my keys and drove over to his apartment.

When I arrived, I stood outside, fidgeting, wondering if meeting him was a good idea. Swallowing hard, I rang the doorbell and waited. I nervously twirled my long black hair around my finger as I waited. A moment later, he opened the door with a happy hello and welcomed me inside.

The apartment was much nicer than I expected for a man who was never home. Soft beige carpet covered the floors giving a warm sense of home. Off-white walls with dark stained trim and baseboards broke up the shades of white. *Supernatural* played on the large television. I knew it well because it was also one of my favorite shows.

I could tell the man I had come to see had been sitting on the dark leather couch. A fading impression of where he was seated remained on the couch. It was an oversized couch built for comfort. The apartment walls were adorned with nice artwork, military memorabilia, and signed posters from movies and television shows. It was enough to make me feel even more nervous.

I was twenty-four years old. He was only six years older but far more accomplished than I was. His accomplishments were displayed everywhere, yet, here I was, still in college and waiting for my life to begin.

He now stood next to me in that Army fatigue uniform, looking like everything a woman would want in an Army man. He was stunningly sexy, like a cross between Hugh Jackman and Gerard Butler, but the uniform made me go weak in the knees. The whole 'man in a uniform fantasy' played out perfectly. I didn't know until later that he would become my soldier, my Sam.

He gave me a sinful smile as he unbuttoned his overshirt, revealing the khaki-colored undershirt beneath that clung to his body, outlining his defined muscular chest. I looked down at his desert jump boots and let my eyes travel up his body to that divine face. Desire ached through me as my eyes drank in his 6'3", body of muscle, with those hungry hazel eyes which never left my body.

My mind seemed to race as he tossed the overshirt over the back of the couch. He took my hand and led me to the couch. We both sat down slowly. I was sure he could tell how

nervous I was. We, after all, had only met after chatting on the internet for months while he was deployed to God knows where, and it truly was God knows where. He was SF, Special Forces; he couldn't tell me if he wanted to. It was part of the mystery that I had come to adore about him.

I probably looked like an idiot sitting there, quiet and nervous as hell, idly playing with his strong fingers. I could feel him watching me curiously.

After a few minutes, he wrapped one of those strong arms around my waist, pulled me against him, and whispered in my ear. "Relax." His voice was like silk to my ears.

I leaned back in his arms, feeling my back supported by his muscular chest. We watched *Supernatural* in silence, but the reality was neither of us was genuinely watching. The tension was still high, but I felt we should be talking. The question was, what do you talk about with a man who can't talk about his job? After jumping out of airplanes and shooting guns at the bad guys, I didn't want to talk about my boring life, which I am sure would seem so trivial to him. I would find out later my trivial life was soothing to him.

He cleared his throat and finally spoke. "How are things with school?" he asked, holding me close as his thumb gently brushed over my stomach.

"It's school. You know, the usual. I think my instructors are morons, but they get paid, and I don't. It's just paper after paper and reading book after book. I wish I would have picked more interesting classes this term," I replied, with the bored tone I usually felt during school.

"Well, it's understandable. I remember there were ones that were always boring. I think that is a requirement for some courses," he replied, chuckling.

"I think so too." I agreed, giggling.

"So…" he paused. "Were all those fantasies you told me about true?" he asked as his hand ran over my stomach and side more firmly than before.

Giggling again as my nerves picked up again. "That was a hell of a transition in conversation!"

"What can I say? You were my sanity during deployment. So, were they?" he asked, smiling as he brushed my hair away from the side of my neck.

"Of course, they were. Were you thinking of one in particular?" I asked, feeling myself getting excited thinking about them.

He leaned in close, and I could feel his warm breath as his lips brushed against my neck. His arms tightened around my waist as if he feared I would run away. I would never run from him.

His lips brushing against my skin made my stomach fill with butterflies of excitement and my body tingle with lust. My hands ran over his as my eyes closed, enjoying his teasing touch.

He began to leave soft kisses on my neck as if they were the shadows of fleeting kisses. He teased me with his kisses as one of his strong hands ran down my thigh wantonly.

His lips drifted up to my ear and whispered. "There are quite a few that have run through my mind. Not just now but during my deployment. They helped me get through a lot of lonely nights."

My breathing got heavier as I thought about him, fantasizing about me. "They did? I would have never thought I was fantasizing material."

He nodded. "Mmhmm."

"Well, do you have a favorite?" I asked softly.

"A favorite?" he said, sitting up a bit. "Hmm… probably

the one where you wanted to be pressed against a wall and kissed like there was no tomorrow, but my mind took it a step or two further." He mused in a husky tone.

"You did?" I asked, surprised. I thought he was so far out of my league.

After a quiet moment, he stood up. "Well, enough of this." He declared, taking my hand and leading me over to the wall. He pushed me against it, not roughly but not gently, either.

At that moment, I wondered if this was his PTSD, causing him to have a flashback, or if this was something else entirely. He looked into my eyes, which I am sure conveyed fear. Though more startling than this were his eyes. I couldn't read them. Perhaps that was his intent.

As shock and confusion coursed through me, what he did next would only heighten my emotions. I was excited, terrified, and wished I knew what he was planning.

He leaned down as his lips pressed against mine, claiming mine in a way I had never felt before. His lips were hot, searing a white-hot passion into the kiss, which melted away every ounce of my nerves. One hand slipped from the right side of my neck into my hair, grasping it gently. He pulled me closer to him as his other hand held the small of my back. His muscular body pressed against mine, pinning me to the wall. I could feel every ounce of his hunger for me.

My arms wrapped around his neck and shoulders holding him close. My hands grasped at his shirt, pulling him closer as if he couldn't be close enough to me. My nerves melted away as lust and passion for him rushed into me.

Desire coursed through us as our tongues caressed each other. Our bodies writhed against each other in lust as our hands wandered and groped. Each touch just added fuel to the fire burning between us.

It seemed like an eternity had passed before he gently broke the kiss. He smiled down at me as I stood still, stunned. "Now, how about we start this afternoon over the right way?" He stated as he gave me a cocky grin.

My mind was a blur of emotions and desire. I met Sam's eyes which were full of devilish yearning. Words escaped me to answer his question. All I had in me clung to him as I gave him a slow nod.

He smiled wider as he leaned in and pressed his lips to mine again. His hand on the small of my back pulled me tighter to him as his other ran up my side and feverously groped my breast.

A soft moan escaped my lips into the kiss as my hands hungrily ran up his chest and around his shoulder. I buried one hand in his hair as the other clung to him.

He pulled my body tight against his as if we were magnets. His hands groped my ass before grabbing my thighs and lifting me up like I weighed nothing.

I opened my eyes and broke the kiss to see where he was carrying me, but his lips never missed a beat as they found my neck again. His kisses were now full-bodied on my neck.

He carried me down the hall without a glance before he turned into a room. His bedroom. He kicked the door closed and laid me down on the bed gently before pulling off his army brown undershirt.

He smiled down at me as he crawled on top of me. "God, you are more beautiful in person. Your pictures didn't do you justice at all," he said, looking into my blue eyes. "They are stunning, but..."

I smile and blush softly before interrupting him. "Must have been a long tour, huh, soldier?" I asked, running my fingers through his hair.

"Impossibly long. I wanted to see you when I walked off the plane, but I was afraid you would think I was rushing things."

I wondered if he had fallen for me during all our long chats. It was hard to believe I was falling for him, too. This meeting just confirmed what I had felt for the last month.

"I will be there next time. I promise. If this is rushing, then don't slow down," I said softly before pulling him to me to kiss him again.

He returned the kiss happily as his hands drifted under my shirt to caress my stomach. The feeling of his manly hand on my soft flesh was exhilarating.

I couldn't even think of how many times I had wished for this during our conversations, or in my fantasies of him after we had talked.

My hands were all too happy to explore his bare chest. Each brush against his skin was as if my fingers were trying to memorize every inch of him.

My mind drifted with the lust and desire that took over me. The world seemed to fade out into a place that was only us.

I knew then that this was only the beginning of our future. This was the start of a chapter of our lives that would change us, and it all started with that first kiss that was now seared into my memory forever.

It had been a week since that glorious day when I met my soldier face-to-face. The Army gave him a month of leave, and he was happy to spend every minute he could with me. I had learned more about him in a week than I had been able to in the months we had chatted online.

Classes were coming to a close for the summer, which would give me more time with him, but finals had started this week. Sadness coursed through me because I knew my time would be spent with my nose in a book, instead of in his arms, or so I thought.

When I heard the knock on my apartment door, I felt anger stir within me because it felt like it was almost ten o'clock, but when I saw it was only seven, my anger subsided a little.

I went to the door dressed in black yoga pants and a red tank top. My long black hair was up in a messy bun.

"Yes?" I said as I opened the door before I could see who it was.

He smiled at me. "Hey…I…hope I am still a welcome visitor?" he asked, concerned about my tone.

I blushed, feeling embarrassment flush through me. "You are always welcome. I am just studying and…" I saw he had several grocery bags in his arms. "What's in the bags?" I asked, perplexed.

"Well, I hoped to be a good boyfriend and cook you dinner while you are studying. Unless you have already eaten?" he asked, kissing me softly before stepping in.

His mention of food made my stomach growl. My hand flew to my stomach as if to silence it. "I haven't eaten since…" I looked up at the clock, "Nine this morning. Did you say, boyfriend?" I asked, closing the door and following him into my kitchen.

"I did. Lyndsey, I love you. Our dates and sleeping together have been wonderful, but now I want the title and to take care of you," he replied, walking over and cupping my cheek.

He sure knew how to make my brain unable to find words. I nodded and smiled happily. "I love you too." My arms wrapped around those wide shoulders as I leaned on my tip toes to kiss those lips now shrouded in scruff.

His lips claimed mine in the most tender fashion that would make most romance authors swoon. My fingers ran through the hair on the back of his head, making him groan with desire for me each time I kissed him.

His kisses were like a drug to me. I never wanted to stop. I would miss them when he had to return to work, and our times together would be limited, but for now, we were both taking full advantage.

As he slowly broke the kiss, he smiled and kept his eyes closed as if he were savoring the kiss.

"I look forward to kissing you every day," he said, opening his eyes.

"They are my favorite part of my days lately," I replied, giving him another quick kiss. "Do you need help cooking?" I asked, adjusting my black-rimmed glasses on my face.

"No, baby. You study. I can find my way around a kitchen," he said, shooing me out of the kitchen. As I turned to go, he called to me. "Baby? I love you in glasses and relaxed. You look sexy as hell."

I blushed deeply and smiled, biting my lower lip before I headed back to my bedroom, where all my books and notes sat scattered on my bed. I crawled back to my spot in the middle of my bed and forced myself to focus on my studies though it was hard knowing he was in my apartment cooking for me.

The sounds of clanking and sizzling with the delicious

smells wafting into the bedroom were more distracting than anything. I grabbed my headphones and turned on Spotify. Music would help me focus, or at least I hoped.

I sat there reading a chapter on the American Revolution when I saw something move out of the corner of my eye. I looked up and pulled out one of my earbuds, only to see him setting a mug of hot tea down on the nightstand.

"I remember you told me you like tea when you read and study. I found a box in your drawer…" he said with a sheepish smile.

"I do. Is there a boyfriend of the year award?" I asked with a sweet smile.

"Nope," he said before leaving me.

Shoving my notes in my book, I closed it, grabbed my tea, and headed into the kitchen. Finding a clear spot on the counter, I hopped up to spend time with him.

"I didn't know you could cook," I said, sipping my tea.

"You never asked. I learned from my mom before she died when I was in high school," he said, smiling over at me as he stirred some kind of sauce.

"I am sorry," I replied gently.

"It's all right. It was years ago. She would have adored you. Pretty sure she would have told me, Sam, you should marry that girl," he said with a smile as he chopped up some bacon.

I giggled and watched him for a moment. He was more amazing than I had ever dreamed. "You know… I have never had a guy treat me like you do or even take care of me." I admitted.

"That's a shame. You deserve it."

"I do?" I asked, surprised.

"Mmhmm. Now, I don't admit what I am about to tell

you easily. I have a big military rep I got to keep up." He began winking over at me. "Deployments downright blow. We hate them. They are dangerous. They are mentally and physically wearing. So, when I would chat and Skype with you, it was my saving grace. Especially when I started falling for you. You kept me safe and sane. It got toward the end where I would miss your smile and voice so much. You have no idea how hard it was for me not to grab you and kiss you when I opened my door…seeing what I have seen makes it hard to sleep and deal at times, but you silence and soothe those demons," he explained while he cooked.

I sat there in shock for a moment. "Wow, and here I keep thinking you are way out of my league…"

"What? No baby, you are out of mine," he said, surprising me again.

"Wow."

"Now, hop down and get your sexy ass to the table. Dinner is done," he said, kissing my cheek before grabbing two plates.

I headed into the dining room, sat down, and watched Sam carry two plates of food, two wine glasses, and a bottle of wine. I looked over the steaks, feeling my stomach growl again. He poured us each a glass before we began to eat.

"So, you have two finals, right, and the rest were papers?" he asked, genuinely curious.

I nodded. "The papers I did before you got home. It is just this history final that is killing me."

"Do you want my help with anything?"

"No, just stay and keep me company?"

"I have a duffle in my truck. I figured that would be easier. You can repack it with some of your stuff if you like."

Things were moving fast from an outside perspective, but

in our world, it was just perfect. We talked more about our favorite things, things we wanted to do together, and what I could expect when he had to go back to work.

After dinner, I helped him clean up before he went to get his duffle. I cleared out a drawer for him and made space for his stuff. I sat on the bed when he walked in with the duffle.

"The top drawer and half of the second are all yours. The left corner of the closet is for your uniforms, and the right corner is for everything else. If that isn't enough space, I can rearrange more."

"If that isn't enough, we would need bigger closets. Though someday we probably will." He implied about moving in together.

"Someday soon, probably," I said, blushing.

He grabbed a book and put it on the nightstand that I didn't use. I saw him remove his tee shirt and undo his belt and jeans. *Now how am I supposed to focus?* I thought as he crawled on my bed.

I grabbed a pair of cotton boy-short panties. I slipped off my yoga pants and stepped into them.

"Now, babe, that's not fair when I know you need to study." He said with a smile as he put one arm behind his head.

"Neither is having you lay there in your boxers," I retorted.

"Fair enough. Come here," he said, motioning to a spot to lie against him and study. He sure didn't know how to play fair.

I laid down, resting my head against his chest as I grabbed my book and began reading, and he did the same.

The warmth and comfort of his arm around me made sleep start to call to me. I fought it the best I could, but dreams of the two of us courting in revolutionary times began to play out in my mind as sleep claimed me.

I would later find out that when my book fell from my hands, he noticed I had drifted to sleep. He gently tucked me into bed, dropping our books on the floor and turning out the lights.

Once the lights were out, he pulled me close and drifted off with me.

When I came home to my apartment after my last day closing out my term, I needed a bottle of Jack and a good cry as I had barely passed my history class. When I left this morning, I left Sam in my apartment, still asleep. I didn't have the heart to wake him to say goodbye, but now I walked in and saw him in the kitchen with a cooler.

"Hey baby, how did it go?" he asked, kissing me softly.

After returning the kiss, I leaned against the counter. "I passed with a C. It was like my brain couldn't remember what history even was, let alone what happened in it," I said softly, feeling discouraged.

He stopped packing the cooler and looked at me, concerned. He grabbed my hips and then made me look at him. "You passed. Damn nerves can make us think we are not worth a damn thing and can get the best of us. No one is going to look at your grades. They are going to look at if you graduated or not," he said, before kissing me and making me smile up at him before continuing. "Listen, I knew you might need an escape, so I planned a little camping trip for us before I have to go back to work next week."

"Camping? I have never been camping…I am not sure I know how to rough it," I said nervously.

"Well, camping for you is more dinner, campfire, and cuddling under the stars - and if you don't want to sleep out there, I made a reservation at a hotel twenty minutes away. Don't you trust me?" he said with a playful smirk.

I couldn't help but giggle and nod. I felt love like I had never felt before.

"What can I do to help?" I asked.

"Go get changed into more appropriate clothes. I will pack the truck up."

I couldn't help but feel the excitement. Sam made my world better no matter how bad it was. I changed into an older pair of jeans, a tee shirt, and hiking shoes. I grabbed my *Supernatural* hoodie and walked out and saw him holding the cooler and a couple of blankets. "I got everything; I think. Ready?" he asked, smiling like he had something else planned.

"Yep," I said, locking up after him.

We headed down to the truck, but when I got in the passenger seat, I glanced at the back seat and saw blankets, pillows, and a bunch of other stuff that was covered up.

I looked over at him when he got in the driver's seat. "Sam, how many days are we going camping?"

"One, maybe two, why?" he asked, starting the truck and pulling out of the parking lot.

"Just a lot of stuff in the back."

He laughed, "You've really never been camping, have you?"

I blushed, "No."

He continued to chuckle before taking my hand and lacing his fingers with mine, "It's okay, babe. I will take care of you."

I smiled, turned up the radio, and leaned back a bit, settling in for the drive out of the city. I sang softly to the music on the radio as he drove past the Army base into the backcountry.

"Have you got to explore much out here?" he asked.

"Not really. I have wanted to, but I was raised in the city, so I don't know much about outdoor stuff except for the occasional day hike."

"Well, I would be happy to show you all of that. My dad and I still take a yearly hunting trip if I have leave time available. We can take you with us if you like," he told me, smiling over at me as he drove.

"Well, I have never been hunting, but sure, you will have to teach me how to shoot. I don't know how to do that either," I said, blushing.

"I got you covered, baby. We will go to the range when I get off work next week." He said, turning and heading deeper on a country road.

"So, where are we headed?" I asked curiously.

"There is this perfect spot out by the lake. Just open enough but far enough away that we are alone," he answered, winking over at me.

"Sounds nice."

"I hope you will love it."

It wasn't long until we descended a trail road and headed around the lake. We turned and drove into an empty field with a view of the lake.

"Now, I am going to get everything set up. You wait here," he said, taking the rear view mirror off the window. "It's a surprise. So, no peeking." He also turned the side mirrors in against the truck before he got out of the truck.

I sat there curious and a little mad. I didn't like surprises, but I turned to look out the back window just as it was covered by a grey material of what I could only think could be a tent. *What on earth is he planning?*

About twenty minutes later, he opened my door. "All set. Ready?" he said with that smile that always made me melt.

I nodded and took his hand as he led me around the back of the truck. A fire was going, and a tent in the back of the truck was full of an air mattress, blankets, and pillows. There was also a table with two chairs, a tablecloth, and candles.

"This is amazing," I said, shocked.

"So, I did well?" he asked, wrapping his arms around my waist from behind.

"Yes. I love it!" I said as his phone began to ring from the truck.

"Damn it, hang on, baby." He let me go and ran to answer it. "Sergeant Rosse? Oh…" he said, walking further away from me. "Not yet. I just am worried it's too soon… Yeah. Okay, thanks." He hung up, turned his phone off, and put it back in the truck. "Sorry about that. Work stuff," He finished walking back over to me.

I sat on the tailgate of his truck. "I understand." I never asked about his work because I knew he couldn't tell me.

He cooked us dinner, and we snuggled by the fire, watching the sunset. When darkness fell, he led me to the truck, and we slipped into the tent and into what nature intended for us.

Three weeks had passed since that night, and life was so blissfully perfect. It was nice being able to write while he was at work and spending the nights in love in each other's arms. The weekends were filled with adventures and romance. He was the best thing to come into my life.

When my parents came to visit, he was the perfect gentleman, making them fall in love with him as much as I had. My dad even told me he would be proud as hell to call him his son-in-law even though we aren't engaged.

Friday had rolled around, and only a few hours stood between us and a romantic weekend at the bay. I sat at my desk writing when my phone chimed with a text.

"Can you meet me on base? Just park outside the gate at the Visitor Center, and I will have one of my guys come pick you up. I want you to come with me to this military thing. Also, could you wear a white dress? Semi-casual or formal or whatever you got will be great. I know it's short notice. My boss told me this morning." Sam texted.

I thought it was odd, but he said stuff like this could happen. I went and looked through my closet for a white dress. When I found one, I tried it on to ensure it still fit. I grabbed my phone and texted back. "Sure, baby. I will be there. The only dress I have that is white is formal. It was my senior prom dress. It still fits, thank God."

A moment later, my phone chimed. "Sounds perfect. I love you. See you in two hours."

I shook my head and went to get ready. I needed to start now if I wanted to be on time. I wanted to look amazing for him.

I put my hair in a braided bun, had a few strands hanging down, and curled them. I figured adding some color wouldn't get him into trouble, so I found my red lipstick and put it on before going and seeing the pair of silver glitter stilettos and slipped into them.

Seeing I had less than an hour to arrive, I grabbed my clutch, phone, and keys and headed out the door. "On my way." I texted him.

As I got in my car, my phone chimed. "Great. Jack is on his way to the gate."

Thirty minutes later, I pulled into the Visitor Center parking lot. I saw a soldier leaning against a Humvee. Once I got out of my car, he ran over to me.

"Lyndsey, right? Sarge talks about you all the time. I'm Jack. Ready to go?" he asked in a polite Southern accent.

"Nice to meet you. Yep, let's go. He sent you in a Humvee?" I asked, surprised.

"Yes, ma'am. You're his girl. He said to treat you like royalty." He said, opening the passenger side door for me.

I laughed. "Sure sounds like Sam. So, what is this thing he is taking me to do?" I asked, fidgeting a bit.

"Don't know, ma'am. It's an officer's thing. But you are dressed to impress," he said, blushing a bit. This guy couldn't have been much older than me.

"Thanks anyway," I replied.

The ride was more interesting as I got to see the base. He drove down the road to what I could only imagine was a large hanger.

"Here we are." He said, getting out, running around to open the door for me, and helping me out. "You are meeting him here." He opened the door to the hanger for me and led me into the small opening. "Go on through that door, ma'am. Nice to meet you," he said with a smile.

I thought the whole thing was strange, but I followed his instructions. As I walked through the door, there was a long hall lined with soldiers on one side, each holding a red lily.

"Welcome, Miss Adams. Just make your way down and

collect your lilies along the way. He will be waiting through the doors at the end of the hall." The first soldier told me as he handed me the first lily.

"What is going on?" I asked, taking it.

"Just go see him." He said with a warm smile.

I nodded and walked slow enough down the hallway accepting each of the lilies and a warm smile from the different soldiers. When I reached the doors, they swung open for me by two more soldiers.

I smiled as I walked into the hangar. There were two helicopters on the ends of the hanger and a tank in the middle. On the top of the tank stood Sam. He smiled at me as the men filed in around me.

"I am an army guy. This has been my first love until I met you. This is my world, or it was until I met you. These guys are the men I command and were my family until I met you." He said before stepping down from the top of the tank. "In these short months, you made all of this mean more and gave me a world to come home to. You are the love of my life, my world, and I want you to become my family." He pulled a black velvet box from his ACU pocket and dropped to one knee before opening it. "Lyndsey, will you marry me?" he asked, looking up into my eyes.

Tears filled my eyes as excitement and love rushed through me like a dam had broken inside me. I looked around in shock, but I was grinning ear to ear in happiness. "Yes..." I whispered, unable to find my voice for a moment. "Yes!" I said louder, finally finding my voice in my emotions.

He put the beautiful princess-cut diamond ring on my finger before picking me up and kissing me as the room erupted in cheers and applause.

As he sat me down and broke the kiss, I saw the army

chaplain walk out from around the tank. “You mean now?!”

He shrugged and nodded, “I was hoping, so if you want to wait, we ca...” I pressed my finger against his lips.

“Now is perfect.”

He kissed me again. “Just let me go change into my dress uniform. Five minutes!” He said, running out of the room.

Not five minutes later, he came running back in, trying to straighten his tie. I couldn’t help but giggle and move his hands away. I straightened it for him and smiled. “Now, I understand why you told me to wear white. Sneaky, sneaky.” I said, smiling.

“You have no idea how many favors I had to call in to pull this off, and that damn ring has been sitting in my pocket for three weeks. I was planning to propose on our camping trip, but I was afraid you would have said no because it was so sudden,” he said, smoothing out his uniform jacket.

“I like you in this one too,” I said, admiring him in his dress uniform.

“Ready?” he asked, blushing a bit.

“Yes,” I replied as he took my hand and handed the bouquet to one of his guys. “Wait, I don’t have a ring for you.”

“Oh, I almost forgot. Your dad sent me this after I asked him for your hand. It belonged to your grandfather.” He said, handing me the golden band engraved with the words my grandmother used to always say about their love. *True love is eternal.*

I smiled and teared up a bit. “I had no idea you were planning all of this. You are amazing! Now, I am ready.” I said before nodding to the chaplain.

“We are gathered here today to bear witness as these two join in marriage. Sam asked me to make this short and

sweet."

"I didn't want her to change her mind," he said as the guys chuckled.

"Lyndsey, do you vow to give all that you are and all that you have to share with Sam? Whatever the future holds, will you love and stand by him as long as you both shall live?" the chaplain asked with a sweet smile.

"I do," I replied, almost bouncing with excitement and love.

"And Sam, do you vow to give all that you are and all that you have to share with Lyndsey? Whatever the future holds, will you love and stand by her as long as you both shall live?"

"Hell yeah! I mean…erhm, I do," he said, correcting himself as he saw his bosses walk in.

"Well then, by the power vested in me, I pronounce you both husband and wife…" he paused, smiling at Sam.

"Well?"

"I just wanted to make you wait for a moment. You may kiss your bride," he chuckled.

Sam growled, then pulled me to him with a happy, passionate kiss. The kiss seemed to stop time for the two of us. The cheers and applause seemed to become a dull roar as our tongues caressed each other.

Two months had gone by since our wedding. We had moved into a lovely house on base and had taken every moment we could to start making a family. We were hopeful but sometimes knew these things take time.

The morning the test had turned positive, my phone rang

with his ringtone. I was so excited to tell him.

"Hey, baby, guess what?!"

"Lyndsey, I don't have much time. They are shipping us out on the next flight. I could be gone for two weeks or six months. I will call you on Skype as soon as I can. They aren't even letting us go home to say goodbye." He said, frustrated.

"Oh… You just keep a clear head and stay safe. Come home to me." I said, trying not to cry.

"I promise I will. I love you so much." His voice broke for a moment.

"I love you too. Go get 'em soldier. I miss you already."

"I will come home soon as I can. Bye, baby. Love you!" he said before hanging up with me.

I set my phone down and cried softly. "Keep him safe. We need him…" I said, praying for the first time since my childhood.

It had been four excruciating months since he was deployed. I hated it; every unknown number on my phone and every car that drove by or slowed down made me worry. I did the only thing I knew he would want me to - focus on our little one instead of worrying.

After putting together the crib, I sat down, attempting to get some writing in as my Skype began to ring. I almost dropped my laptop out of my lap.

"Sam?" I answered.

"Hey, baby! I am sorry I haven't gotten to call you before now. Shit is crazy here. How are you? Are you okay?" he asked, dusty and sunburned but looking like the man I married.

"It's okay. I am good now. Any idea when you are coming home?" I said, setting my laptop on my growing belly.

"In a couple of months, maybe sooner. We have no real idea yet. I only have a couple of minutes. My guys are anxious to call their spouses too. I just needed to see your beautiful face for a minute. I love you so much! God, I miss you!"

"I know you have to go, but you keep a clear head, you hear me? Come home soon. I love you, baby!"

"I love you too! Got to go, baby! Love you!" he said, blowing me a kiss.

I blew him one back just as the screen said, 'Call ended.'

Tears rolled down my cheeks. At least I knew he was alive and safe for the moment, but it was hard to be away from him. I wiped my tears away and rubbed my belly before entering the nursery and unpacking the baby stuff I had bought. It was the only thing to calm me.

A month later, I was walking in the door when my phone started to ring. Frantically digging, I finally found it and answered it.

"Hello?"

"Mrs. Rosse?" the female voice asked.

"Yes?" I said, feeling my heart stop hoping this wasn't that call.

"I am calling about your husband, First Sergeant Samuel Rosse. He has been shot. He is alive and has made it through surgery and will need someone to pick him up tomorrow at the command hanger at 1 pm."

I stifled a sob, "God, you should have led with he was alive! I will be there at noon waiting for him."

"I am sorry, ma'am. He cussed me this morning when I didn't call you when he first arrived. But I have learned it's better to get cussed only once."

"Yeah. Thanks, bye." I said, hanging up. I grabbed my keys and purse and headed back into town.

I wanted to find a new dress to wear for him and one that would fit this belly.

The next day I sat in the waiting room watching for that plane to land. I needed him.

I must have zoned out, because before I realized a soldier was tapping me on the shoulder. "Ma'am, they are coming off the plane now."

I quickly stood up and startled out. "Thank you!"

He chuckled and waved me off.

I walked out to the fence and waited for him. So many soldiers I saw walking off the plane, but not him. I saw six soldiers carrying a casket, and my heart sank.

Tears filled my eyes, but then I saw the last one walk off the plane in a sling. It was him. It was my Sam. They saluted the coffin before the soldiers carried it into the hangar. He turned and dismissed his men before walking toward me. I moved my coat from in front of me and draped my arm to show him my pregnant belly.

He stopped for a moment before he ran over to me. He grabbed me and kissed me hard and passionately.

"You are pregnant?! Why didn't you tell me?" His hands held my belly, and tears began to roll down his cheeks.

"I was going to tell you when you told me you were leaving. I wanted you to have a clear head. I didn't want you distracted, and you still got shot." I said, gently touching his shoulder.

"We were ambushed. I was lucky most of us made it out alive. Many of us were injured. Jack…the young soldier you met on our wedding day, was the one we lost," he said, taking my hand and leading me through the hanger. "They are discharging me. I get to be a recruiter, or I can teach. At least, that is what they are offering. The damn bullet did too much damage."

I would never admit how relieved I was, but I knew he would be a recruiter over a teacher. After all, the Army was his first love.

"Do you know if it is a boy or a girl?" he asked, smiling.

I smiled, "A boy and a girl."

"Twins?!"

"Yes, sir."

"Let's go home, baby. I have some time to make up for." he smirked.

Raven Child

Awaken my little raven child.
Open your eyes and follow your wings.
Yet your mind is so curious and brave.
Always seeking and learning,
Yet, each answer is never enough.
You fly to new adventures,
In the wilds of your heart.
To rich deep green mountain forests,
Following a path toward groves of Fae.
Or to the top of snow-capped mountains,
That leads you to dragon-filled caves.
Then finding the road to the Kingdom of Stuffies,
Only then to find the Gardens of Magic.
But don't stray too far, little raven child,
Though we can always hear your calls of joy,

You are always needed at home,
No matter how far your heart will travel.
From Fae to dragons, to Stuffies, and more,
Keep a close watch for the candle by the door.
A light to guide you, my little raven child,
When the time has come for you to come home.

By Brittany L. Adkins & J.T. Baxter

The village was absolutely buzzing today. The King was visiting. Many of the towns in the kingdom would see a visit from the King each year for his hunting trips. After a successful hunt, he was known for being a generous king, leaving gold in the streets. However, each town he visited was left with a strangeness, and some local maidens would go missing.

The day the king arrived, all citizens were to line up and welcome him. Deyanira was no exception to this law. She was a young maiden of twenty-one and one of the darlings of the village. Like the other citizens, she bowed when he got off his horse and looked around at the people. He looked over each citizen as if he were searching for someone when his gaze stopped on her. It was as if he looked her over like a prized horse at auction. A smile crept over his stern face. His smile was chilling, yet something inside her wanted to see it again. The King nodded to his man and pointed to her. Though the town was quietly awaiting their dismissal from the King, no one could hear the brief, hushed discussion between the King and his captain. With a quick nod, the captain turned and began to order his men to prepare things for the King. The King smiled and waved his hand, dismissing the townspeople.

The next afternoon, Deyanira was feeding her family's goats just outside her home when four of the king's soldiers approached her.

"Girl! His Majesty would like to see you." one said from behind the helm that covered his face.

"Me, my lord?" she replied, looking for confirmation.

"Now." he said firmly as he grabbed her arm, making her drop the bucket of grain on the ground.

"Owww! Of course, I will go, but you don't have to grab me!" She tried to pull from his grasp, but it was too firm.

He forced her toward the king's tent, making her stumble, but she didn't fall. As four of his heavily armored guards escorted her to the king's tent, she noticed the townspeople quickly heading into their homes as if some knew things she didn't. She was so young the last time the king visited, so she didn't remember the townspeople acting this way.

Upon arriving at the tent, the gruff guard forced her inside, making her stumble to her knees before the king. She bowed her head and then looked up at him.

"Have I done something wrong, Your Majesty?" she asked softly.

The King laughed and helped her up. "Not at all, my dear. My guards are a little rough, but they are good for protection. You aren't hurt, are you? I wouldn't want your beautiful body to be spoiled for our time together," he said as he ran his hands down over her body.

Deyanira realized at that moment why the king had called for her. He desired her for his bed. She blushed and shook her head. "No, Your Majesty. I am unharmed. It is an honor to be here with you."

He smiled and began to circle around her. "You understand why you are here?"

She nodded. "For your bed," She said nervously.

He let out a dark laugh. "I do not fuck in my bed with common pretty things like you. I fuck in the wilds. Now go out to the woods like a good whore for me and take that dress off and wait. I will fuck you when I get there." He said as his hands groped her body.

Deyanira knew she had no choice in the matter. She nodded, pulled from his lustful grasp, and headed out to the woods. Once she stepped into the woods, she felt as if there were eyes all around her. Many hunters only ventured into the woods for hunting but never anything else. The woods were home to various creatures and monsters. She began to undress fully and looked around for him as she stood naked, waiting. Part of her did not want to be claimed by the king, but the other part was so thrilled to be chosen it aroused her. In truth, no one says no to the king. His temper was not one to anger.

After several dragging minutes, she heard footsteps. He had arrived.

"My, my, what a beauty you are," he said as his fingers brushed over her long brown locks.

His hands traveled down her chest to her full breasts, and his hand squeezed one softly before moving further. Her slender but voluptuous waist was his next target. Both hands grasped her sides, firmly pulling her to him.

"You are almost so perfect I wish I could keep you," he said before one hand slipped down between her full thighs. "Aroused and ready for your King. I am not yet, and I want to play a little before I take what I need. I like to chase my prey," he said in her ear. "The appropriate term would be hunt my prey. If you outrun me, you will be fucked and bred like a good village whore. If you don't…well, no one will miss you. You may have a few moments head start," he said, pushing her away as a guard appeared with a bow. "Run, little girl. Run!"

She watched him pull out an arrow and nock it in his bow before she realized he was serious. She gasped and began to run barefoot through the woods. "Help me! Please! Help me!" she screamed.

"They know better than to help you, you little bitch!" the king called after her as he shot an arrow in her direction.

She heard the arrow hit a tree. She screamed louder as she ran painfully through the forest.

Osteus paused with his hand on the door to the inn. He let out a soft sigh. *Was this a good idea?* As he walked into the small village, he had already received several unpleasant looks. His spear was propped up against the wall of the inn. He was imposing enough without walking into a room full of people wielding a spear. He turned the handle and entered the inn, dodging immediately as a pewter jar smashed into the doorframe beside him. He looked down at the broken receptacle and then up at where it originated. The burly man behind the bar was glowering at him.

"You're not welcome here, abomination! Get out!" Osteus tightened his grip on the hilt of the sword sheathed at his belt. His nostrils flared as he surveyed the interior of the inn. A small voice in the back of his mind spoke to him. *They will revile you Osteus. Just remember, you are unique, and you deserve life.* He smiled inwardly. His mother had been a wise woman. Osteus removed his hand from the hilt of his sword and held up his palms.

"I mean no harm," he said softly. "I am simply looking for work you may have." The inn-keep kept his face stern and demanding.

"You are not wanted here," he hissed through his teeth. "Be gone!"

Osteus sighed and backed out the door, knowing better than to turn his back on any threat. Once he closed the door behind him and stepped back into the blazing midday sun, he looked around the village. He was still receiving looks from everyone there. It did not surprise him. His half-satyr, half-faun heritage lent him no favors. He was despised in every place he went. He turned south and headed for the woods. The heat was making him sweat, and he needed to bathe. Heading for the pool nearest his small domicile, he watched as the village gave way to the nature of the woods. Creatures, great and small, permeated the woods that he had called home for the past several years. The sounds and smells of nature filled his senses, and he smiled. Peaceful. It was peaceful here, away from man and their problems. He reached the pool and heard laughter coming across the wind. He could not help but smile a little more. As he pushed through the bushes, he saw them. The three water nymphs that frequented this pool sat on rocks surrounding it as they talked and laughed.

They paused as Osteus approached; their gaze wary. He could not blame them. He was a half-satyr, and satyrs did not have a good reputation with the nymphs. He slowly bowed to them, and they relaxed, motioning to the pool of water. He smiled and began to remove his weapons and armor. Moments later, he removed his clothes and set them all down within reach of the pool. Then, he slowly lowered himself into the waters. The pool was warm, heated by the midday sun, and the magic of the nymphs who now sat only feet away from him. Osteus scooped water into his hands and began to wash his body. His heritage gave him a unique appearance. He retained his mother's goat legs and soft facial features, but the rest came from his father. The strong horsetail, the large, firm horns atop his head, and his dominating, untamed nature that took over him more than he liked all belonged to his father.

Osteus was nearly finished bathing when a shrill scream pierced the air. Birds exploded from nearby trees, and the nymphs dove below the water's surface, down the tunnel he knew was deep below. He climbed out of the pool and dressed quickly in his armor, strapping on his sword, and picking up his spear before rushing through the woods in search of the source of the scream.

Deyanira could feel cuts on her bare feet as she ran. She screamed and ducked into a thicket only to feel an arrow graze her arm. She let out a cry of pain and kept running. Exiting the thicket, she looked behind her to see the king drawing another arrow. As she turned to find a way to hide, she crashed into something large.

She looked up right into the gleaming eyes of one of the woodland creatures. He looked like a satyr or a faun, but all she could do was scream and try to escape him as another arrow hit the tree next to them. She felt the creature grab her firmly but gently.

"Oh, little girl, I am growing so aroused. I think it's time to see if you bleed," he called to her. "I will find you. I always find my prey, and you will bleed for me."

Deyanira looked up at the creature that held her. She looked panicked but had no option but to hope for help.

"Help me…he is hunting me…please…" she begged in a terrified whisper.

Osteus' head snapped up from the girl who clung to him now to the band of men rushing through the woods, obviously chasing her…no, hunting her, as she said. The group stopped in their tracks as they beheld the massive satyr that stood before them, their prey clinging to it like it would save her life.

"Beast! Be gone from here!" shouted the man who was clearly in charge of the group. He wore fine clothes and a crown. In his hand was a bow, an arrow nocked on the string. "That girl is mine!" he exclaimed.

Osteus glared at the group. He could feel the satyrian rage coursing through him. Anger, fire, bloodlust. These men would not survive their encounter with him. The powerful satyr launched his spear toward the group without letting go of the girl at his side. The deadly missile hit true, skewering one of the men beside the leader and forcing him backward, pinning him to a tree. Osteus counted quickly. One down, four to go. He looked down at the girl and softly moved her arm from around him. Her arm did not even reach all the way around his body. She was small and delicate. He motioned to the tree behind him.

"Wait there," he told her, his voice gruff and commanding. She nodded slowly, her eyes still wide as she moved to the tree and leaned against it, her breath returning to her after the exhausting sprint through the woods.

Osteus unsheathed his sword from his belt, the polished iron catching the sunlight that pierced the canopy of leaves above them.

The leader of the group was red-faced as he looked back at the man Osteus had impaled to the tree.

"Fucking beast! You will die for this!" He screamed as he brought his bow up and loosed the arrow. Faster than what seemed possible for a beast of his size, Osteus deflected the arrow with his sword, his lightning reflexes taking the group aback. The leader nocked another arrow. "KILL HIM!" he shouted at his men. The other three already had their weapons out: two swords and one battle-axe. Osteus smiled as he took a fighting stance and waited. As he predicted, all three men charged him. But there was an order to their charged assault. The two with swords charged him first, coming at both his flanks while the man with the battle axe ran at him head-on.

Osteus swung his sword in a gigantic arc in front of him, catching both swordsmen with the move and instantly disemboweling them. They dropped to the ground, dead. The third man had stopped his charge before Osteus' sword came close to him, and now he stood in shock, his eyes fixated on the dead bodies of his comrades. Osteus flicked his sword, blood from the two dead men splattering to the ground. He then turned his attention to the man with the battle axe.

"I will give you *one* chance to live," he said, his eyes boring into the man's. "Drop your weapon and leave…or die." The man visibly paled, but his grip tightened on his axe. Osteus raised an eyebrow. Brave man. Foolish, but brave. The axe-wielding man screamed a war cry and swung his weapon at the satyr. Osteus dropped to one knee, the blow swinging clear over his head as he thrust forward his sword, impaling the man through the chest. The crack of the man's ribs as the sword broke them was audible, and he coughed once, blood bubbling from his mouth. Osteus retracted his blade, and the man collapsed beside his two comrades. Only then did Osteus become aware of the arrow protruding from his left arm. He looked back to the leader, who was frantically searching for another arrow in his quiver. Osteus roared, an almighty beastly sound, and the man shot his gaze back to the satyr. Then, unexpectedly, he turned and ran. He ran so fast that Osteus thought Hermes himself was carrying him. The satyr watched until he was out of sight and then laughed, snapping the arrow in his arm off, leaving just a small section lodged in his arm. He would deal with that later. The grass near him rustled, and he turned to see the girl, no…the young woman, walking gingerly toward him. He wiped his sword off on one of the fallen men's tunics and then sheathed the weapon, holding up his hands to her.

"Do not fear me," he said in his commanding voice.

She nodded as she stepped closer. It was then that his nostrils filled with the smell of more blood, and he looked down. Her feet were bare and bleeding. His eyes slowly moved up her body. She was bare everywhere. He sighed and took a step closer to her. She looked like she was about to step back but stood firm. Surprisingly, she allowed him to take her into his arms, and he cradled her against his chest, her wounded feet hanging over one of his arms. Then he turned and headed back to the pool.

Deyanira clung to the beast so tightly she was sure she was hurting him. She let out a soft sob as she realized she was safe. At least safer than when she was running from the King.

She buried her face against him, terrified to let go.

Soon, she felt him lean down and sit her carefully on the bank of the pool. It took her a moment to loosen her grip on him.

"I know I shouldn't trust you, but please…don't leave me?" she said, looking up at him. Her voice was hoarse from her screams and still riddled with fear.

She felt hands gently grasp her ankles, making her jump and gasp. She looked down to see two nymphs gently pulling them into the water.

"We won't hurt you. Let us help." One of the nymphs said with a gentle and soothing voice.

"You…won't? Don't you steal humans?"

The two nymphs giggled. "No, that's a silly myth made by humans. We will help you."

Deyanira nodded and looked back at the sizeable satyr-like creature. She didn't understand why she didn't want to leave his side. Her instincts told her to run, but the very thought made her want to cry as if her heart was breaking. She met his eyes. They were gentle despite the horror she had just witnessed at his hands.

"Thank you. I can never repay what you did. But I also know I can never go back. The King will have me killed." She tried to stifle a sob, but it was no use. Her tears flowed freely.

Osteus sighed as he knelt beside her. He winced as the adrenaline in his system started to wear off, and he felt the throbbing in his arm where the arrow shaft was still lodged.

"You have nothing to fear here," he told the young woman. "I am sorry you had to witness what happened back there, but those men deserved nothing less than death." He began to remove his armor, the bronze chest plate that covered his torso, stylized as if it had muscles of its own.

When he removed it, his body had the same muscles as the armor. He wore no greaves or sandals, his goat legs offering more than enough protection. All that was left was his waistband, the strips of cloth covered with leather tassets that protected his nether regions. He suddenly became painfully aware that the woman in front of him was naked, and the sight of her now in this peaceful situation made his arousal grow. He felt himself harden beneath his waistband, but he could do nothing about it. He had to get into the pool to clean his wound and the grime of the battle from his body. He sighed and removed the waistband, his cock springing free as he did so. This was another characteristic of his father's side. Although his mixed heritage meant he was not in a permanent state of erectness like all other male satyrs, he had inherited the enlargement common to them. He sank into the water, thankful that it was still warm, and slowly worked on healing his wounded arm. It then dawned on him that he had no idea who this woman was or why she was being chased.

"What is your name?" he asked her gently. "And why were those men chasing you?"

Deyanira blushed, seeing how handsome his body was. She also noticed how his body responded to what she could only assume was her nakedness, making her blush deeper.

"The King takes women as lovers from each village he visits on his hunts. Now…I realize why his lovers have not returned. It was presumed he took them home…no, he kills them. He wanted me to be his prey, as he called it," she replied as she felt the nymphs pull her into the water to clean the scratches and wounds on the rest of her body. "I am Deyanira…my name is Deyanira. What is yours? Also, what do you plan to do with me?" she asked as the nymphs guided her deeper into the pool closer to him.

"My name is Osteus," he replied gruffly. He seemed lost in thought for a moment. "And I have no plans to do anything with you. You screamed for help, and I helped."

Deyanira knew the legends and knew Fauns were kind and lustful but not as lustful as Satyrs. Satyrs could be cruel and fearsome, and their lust knew little boundaries. Yet here he was, and he was her savior. He looked like a mixture of the two.

As her eyes traveled over his body, they stopped at the arrow he had taken for her. Her small hand gently touched the wood still protruding from his arm. It was a delicate touch.

"I can help remove this if you will allow me. It is my fault you have it," she said in her almost hoarse whisper.

He felt her hand on his arm and paused, looking down at her as she sat in the pool, the nymphs cleaning her wounds. The warmth of her hand on his arm was…pleasant. It had been a long time since he had been touched by anyone. He realized he had been staring at her and had not answered her.

"I would appreciate your help," he told her.

He spoke as she started to work on removing the arrow from his arm.

"What your king did, there is no honor in that. A man with such power should not be allowed to abuse it." He winced as she pulled the arrow from his arm, and blood started to flow freely into the pool.

He wrapped a bandage from his pack around his arm, tight enough to staunch the flow of blood. It was then he caught her glancing at his hardened cock beneath the water. He felt himself stir, and he smirked a little. His blood began to boil, not with anger, but with arousal. The primal nature of the satyr and the softer side of the faun in him fighting for dominance. His eyes roved over her body. Her full breasts were large for her slender form, but her waist and hips were curved, making her entire body a beautiful sight to behold. His cock twitched in the water, and he saw her cheeks redden as she noticed the movement.

She had an overwhelming desire to be close to him. She felt her hands slip up his chest as she stood before him. Her eyes traveled up until they met his. She slowly pulled her hands away from his body as she realized how intimate she was getting with him.

"Is this some sort of satyr magick? I have this overwhelming feeling in me to be close to you. I should be afraid of you…all the legends of your kind say you are not safe for humans. But I don't want to leave your side…" she said, clasping her hands together so she wouldn't give into her desires.

He looked at her with concern despite his burning need to take her.

"There is no magick at work here, at least…not any that I am doing willingly. But I also have this desire, more so than just to have you…but to be yours, to claim you." He paused as he felt himself twitch again. Then it hit him.

"There is a legend of fated mates," he told her softly. "A bond so powerful that it transcends all others. Could that be what this is?" he asked out loud, more so to himself than to her. He moved his hands slowly and rested them on her waist. His hands were so massive that he could wrap them around her entire waist if he wanted to. *Could they truly be fated mates?* Him, a satyr and faun hybrid, and her, a human. His eyes moved from hers down to what lay between her thighs. It didn't even seem possible that he could fit inside her. The thought burned through him, and he shook his head.

She felt his hands on her waist. His touch was like oxygen to a flame. She needed more. Her hands returned to his chest as she hesitantly let them slip over his shoulders.

"I have heard those stories, but I always assumed they weren't real…" she began as she felt him pull her closer to him. "Osteus…" she said his name almost as a moan as she felt her breasts press against his chest. "How do we know for sure?" she asked as she licked her lips.

The fear was gone from her body, and the pain was fleeting from the warm, soothing waters. But her arousal and desire to be his were growing rapidly. She couldn't understand how this creature, whom many would call a monster, longed to be hers.

His name on her lips was like nectar from the Gods, and he moaned softly as she pressed her breasts against his chest. He could feel her nipples pebbled against his muscles, making his cock ache for her. He looked into her eyes.

"I think the fact that you're so ready, so willing to be close to me, even though all logic says you should stay away, is proof enough," he told her. "There is something, some force, making us feel this way. There has to be." He moved his hands down and cupped her ass, slowly lowering her to sit in his lap. He groaned as he felt her soft folds rub down his shaft. She was wet, so very wet, and not from the waters of the pool. He gritted his teeth as he felt his lust taking over. All he wanted was to impale her on his cock right there and then, but he didn't want to hurt her. He wanted her to be his, in every sensual and feral way possible, but he would never hurt her purposefully…at least, not unless she asked him to. His head swam with the thoughts, and before he knew what he was doing, his lips were on hers. The kiss was hard and passionate, but also caring and meaningful. She would not be just a fuck to him. She was meant for him. This he knew down to his very core.

"Deyanira…" he moaned into their kiss.

Lust and desire filled her body as if his kiss was the spark that started the wildfire between them. She wrapped her arms around him as much as she could as the feeling of this thick cock pressed against her folds. Hearing him say her name was like hearing Aphrodite's blessing of their union.

"Please Osteus…I want to be yours, please…" she begged against his lips.

She could feel his strong hands grasp her body and gently begin to guide her down on his cock.

Osteus groaned with pleasure. The tip of his cock found her entrance. He cursed inwardly, knowing he was too big for her. The satyr heritage was a curse in this sense. He looked into her eyes.

"Deyanira…this…this might hurt at first," he told her. She caressed his cheek and nodded as she kissed him back. He felt her tongue brush his, and he tightened his grip on her body ever so slightly as he pushed her down onto his cock. He moaned into their kiss, and he heard her gasp in pain. He paused, but she smiled and nodded, a silent plea for him to continue. He did so. Her pussy was so tight, so very, very tight around the thickness of his cock, that he was afraid he was going to hurt her. But then he heard her moans. He felt her wetness coat his cock as she enveloped him, and he growled. And unexpectedly, he was there, at the very bottom of her. He had filled her all the way to the entrance to her womb, his cock buried inside her like they were meant to fit together. The feeling was beyond words.

"Fuuuuck," was all that escaped his lips as his head rolled

backward, feeling her tight wetness surround him. "You feel incredible," he told her, his breath catching with every minute movement either of them made.

She knew it would hurt, but Gods above, she would have given her soul to Hades to feel him in her like this. She would desire to feel him like this for the rest of her days.

She let out a loud, lustful moan as she rolled her hips slowly. The pleasure was almost overwhelming. She buried her face against his neck as she felt his hands guiding her in a slow and intimate rhythm. She held onto him tightly as they claimed each other.

"I know you are trying to be kind and gentle for me, but I can feel the struggle within you…I don't know how, but I can. I trust you. Claim me how you need. I give you permission…my mate…" the word mate rolled off her tongue like she had said it a million times before. She kissed him again, feeling like a tether had formed between them. She could feel his desire, his longing for her, and dare she say, his love.

Osteus' eyes widened at her words. His breath caught, and he growled deeply in his throat. This woman had just offered herself to him, had called him her mate, and told him to claim her. He had been holding back. He didn't want to hurt her, but he knew he needed to claim her as his. He looked into her eyes, put his hand to her cheek, and smiled.

"You are mine, Deyanira," he growled, and then, he took her. He wrapped his hands around her waist, holding her before he started to bounce her on his cock, not slow and delicately, but fast and deep, every movement forcing his cock to fill her again and again. He cursed as his breath hitched.

"By the gods!" he exclaimed as he felt her pussy grip his

cock every time he entered her. She was moaning loudly now, the woods filled with the sounds of their ecstasy. The nymphs had long departed the pool, and even the wildlife around them seemed to be keeping a distance away, respecting the sanctity of their union.

His cock throbbed inside her, and his heart beat faster and faster. It had been years since he'd had any woman, never mind one as beautiful as the one he held in his hands now. He moved out of the water, his cock still buried inside her, and sat down on the bank at the edge of the pool. Now, he could feel her wetness dripping down his shaft as she bounced on it repeatedly. The feeling of her around him was something he never wanted to let go of. Then he felt it, the surge in his balls, the warning that orgasm was close. He held onto her, his grip tightening as he looked into her eyes. She met his eyes, and they both knew what was happening. She nodded to him.

"Do it, Osteus, breed me, my mate."

He lost all control. He roared as his orgasm ripped through him, and he thrust up into her while bringing her down on him. The tip of his cock pressed against her womb, and cum exploded from his cock, his balls pumping and pumping the hot, thick liquid into her waiting womb. His entire body tensed as the orgasm took hold of him, and he became keenly aware that so much of his cum was leaking out of her, down his cock and balls, and onto the ground beneath them.

She hadn't stopped. She couldn't. She wasn't ready to come, not yet. She desired to feel him just a moment longer. She continued to bounce hard on his cock as she felt her pussy begin to tighten around his thick cock. She tossed her head back in pleasure as she grabbed his horns. Her moans and cries of pleasure could be heard at a distance as she felt her orgasm explode, drenching his cock in her juices.

Her pace began to slow after a few moments, only for her to see him smiling wickedly at her. She blushed and leaned in to kiss him, only to feel his hand slip around her throat.

"Not yet, my love. First, I must hear those cries again." He said, lifting her off his cock and laying her on the soft moss of the bank and moving down between her thighs. "I need to taste what is mine and only mine."

Deyanira blushed and spread her legs wide for him, presenting herself to him fully. She would give him the world if she could, but for now, she would give herself to him. She watched as he grasped her legs and pulled her up to his awaiting lips.

His eyes met hers as he placed a soft kiss on her mound. "When I am finished, every creature in Greece will know you belong to me."

He felt her pulse against his lips as he kissed her again, and then, he opened his mouth and ran his strong tongue down her slit, parting her folds with the muscle as he went down. The moan from her was loud, and he felt it through her entire body. Osteus smiled at her response to his tongue, and slowly, he teased her, stroking it up and down her folds, parting them ever so slightly, and pushing the tip into her entrance before withdrawing it. He noticed the small button above her mound quivering, and a wicked grin crossed his face. He closed his mouth over her clit and sucked once before using his tongue to circle it, flicking and feeling her buck slightly at the sensation. He held her legs down, his strength pinning her to the ground, unable to move, entirely at his mercy. He moaned against her clit, the vibration causing her to buck more before he took his mouth off her and looked into her eyes.

"You are mine, Deyanira," he growled as he plunged his tongue inside her dripping cunt. She screamed, and he paused for a second before realizing it was a scream of pleasure as his tongue stretched her. Admittedly it was not as big a stretch as his cock had been, but the feeling was undoubtedly intense for her. His tongue was by far more muscular and firmer than a human's. He guessed to her it would feel almost like a human cock. She moaned loudly as he swirled his tongue inside her, tasting her insides for the first time and realizing the taste on his tongue was a mixture of both their orgasms. Combined, they were sweet—definitely the nectar of the Gods.

There was no stopping him, nor did she want him to. His tongue was something the Gods must have spent ages perfecting. She reached down and grasped his horns, pulling him deeper into her. Her legs were locked in his tight grasp. It would have been impossible to escape him, not that she ever wanted to.

"Great Gods! Osteus! Do not stop!" she cried out to the heavens as he continued devouring her like she was his last meal.

A low, rumbling growl escaped his lips as he looked up at her, and his grip tightened almost painfully on her thighs. He had no intentions of stopping until he was covered in her juices like a proud warrior covered in blood. His tongue penetrated her deeply, driving her wild with every thrust. As her pussy tightened around him, he knew it wouldn't be long until he would have his desire.

Deyanira screamed out as she bucked against him. Her orgasm burst free from her with a force she had never known, making her shudder in his hands. She felt him pull his tongue back and lap up every savory drop of her gently, allowing her to come down from the heavens. He chuckled as she finally let go of his horns and allowed him to look at his mate in all her spent glory.

"You are the most beautiful creature I have ever laid my eyes upon. I don't know if I have ever felt love before for anyone outside of my family, but for you, my sweet little lamb, I dare say I love you," he proclaimed.

Deyanira blushed as she panted still from the beastly orgasm he had just given her. "I love you too. It feels as if I have loved you forever."

Osteus smiled as he let go of her thighs and slowly leaned down to kiss her. Their lips met, and the kiss was soft and loving. He carefully picked her up from the ground and carried her back into the pool, this time to wash the aftermath of their sex away. He softly and caringly cleaned her as they sat together in the pool. It was early evening now. They had been at the pool for longer than he had thought, but the water remained warm; no doubt thanks to the nymphs.

After several minutes of cleaning, the pair got out of the pool. Osteus began to dress in his clothes and armor and then became painfully aware that Deyanira had no clothes. She had left them behind in the woods when the king had ordered her to remove them. He sighed softly and picked her up in his arms.

"I'm going to take you back to my home. I may have some clothes you can wear, and we can figure out what happens now," he told her. She nodded as she lay in his arms, grateful he had opted to carry her as her feet, while healing from the nymph's ministrations, still stung from the cuts she had sustained while being chased.

Not long after they left the pool, they entered a small clearing deeper into the woods. A small hut constructed of wood and stone stood there. There was a small garden on one side of the hut, and what looked like a small blade-sharpening wheel tucked under an awning on the other side of the hut.

Osteus shouldered open the door and walked inside carrying Deyanira. The inside was sparse but cozy. A small fireplace was set into one wall, embers charring the last pieces of wood. A bed large enough to hold a beast of Osteus' size was against another wall. He carried her to the bed and sat her down gently before rummaging through a pile of clothes at the foot of the bed. He pulled out a large shirt and sniffed it quickly before handing it to her. She gratefully accepted it and pulled it over her naked body, shivering slightly. He looked back at the fire and proceeded to add more logs to it, stoking it with the iron poker at the side. The fire roared to life in minutes, and he remained there, hunched over it, his goat legs supporting his massive frame.

Deyanira scooted off the bed and came to sit beside him on a stool near the fire. She held her hands out to feel the fire, and it was not long before the warmth filled the hut.

She finally looked up at him. "My love…what will happen now? I have never dreamed of being someone's love, let alone someone's fated mate. Most humans marry for money, land, or titles. It is rare to marry for love. It seems I'm saying it out loud and feeling how I feel towards you… Humans may be more of the monsters than the beasts of the land."

Osteus listened to his mate before getting down to her level. "My little lamb. Some humans are evil. Your King is one. But…here you are, the lady of our home. I will protect you and love you so fiercely that Hades will question if it is the right choice to take you on the day when you pass from my arms. But until that day, I will give you all of me. You are home and safe. Everything else is just small details we will work out," he said before reaching up and caressing her cheek with his strong hand.

Deyanira leaned forward and kissed her mate with all the love within her.

Summer had faded, and the changing of the leaves showed Persephone's descent back to her mate. Deyanira stepped out of the small hut carrying a tankard of warm cider for Osteus as he chopped wood for their home.

"My love, take a break. Winter is not at our heels yet," she called to him as his ax swung down once more, splitting the large log.

"By the Gods, you grow more beautiful with each passing day." He took the tankard and drank it down before giving a hearty laugh. "You spoil me. This is divine."

Deyanira smiled and kissed him. "I am just a blessed woman."

He lifted her off the ground and kissed her deeply again. "We both are blessed."

Osteus had been an outcast most of his life, but these past few months with Deyanira had shown him he was everything to someone. He was not a monstrous beast to her. She had shown him he was worthy of love.

Deyanira's days were filled with love and passion as Osteus kept his promises to her. Though she was never able to return home, she had shown another neighboring village that Osteus was a worthy ally, and many came to trust him.

Fate and monstrosity had brought them together, but in the end, they were happier than ever.

Snow

March has arrived
Yet, the specks of lace fall from the sky.
The brush of the icy breeze caresses my skin,
Compelling me to watch
The white specks fall from above.
But the chill of the breeze passes through me
As if it is a spirit of Winter's clutching hold.
Despite the spirit's frozen push
Compelling me to retreat inside,
To the warm refuge,
I walk out under the fall
And tilt my head up to the heavens.
The lace stings as it touches my flushed face,
As if it is made from unseen blades,
Meant to harm all that it touches.
My ears only hear the eerie silence,

As the world grows quiet under its frozen coating.
I look around as the silence makes
The spirit's call through the trees more frightening.
"Why?" I ask myself in a whisper.
"It is beautiful, but why does it strike fear?"
Silence makes the heart grow louder,
A sound we rarely hear.

My Demon

The wind was cold, and the sky was an eerie grey, giving this place an ominous feel. As I got out of my car, I realized this was, by far, the craziest thing I had ever done. I looked around, seeing the effect of late autumn on the trees. The wind blew leaves around me as if telling me to get back into my car, drive away, and never look back. The thing is, I don't get scared that easily. I grabbed my keys, closed my car door, and approached the large manor. It had been restored for me, but that didn't make it any less creepy. Unlocking the door, it creaked as if I were in a scary movie.

One by one, I turned on the lights and looked around, seeing the beautiful Victorian home come to life. I made my way up the stairs as I explored my new home. I suppose old houses like this should have a history or ghosts of memories that haunt them, but those would feel different from what I felt. I didn't feel alone. That feeling in your gut just tells you someone or something else is here.

Walking down the large hallway at the top of the stairs, I heard the floorboards creak and groan from the master bedroom, confirming my suspicions. All I could think about was how stupid I was to move into a large manor twenty miles from the nearest town, but I inherited it from a crazy great uncle I met once. It sounds even more stupid now that I am thinking about it. Women in horror movies die every day doing stupid things like this, yet here I am.

Walking down the hall, I could feel my stomach knot up as my heart raced in my chest. *I should run and call the cops…What am I doing? I am not this brave!* I thought, despite my feet still carrying me forward. Curiosity told me I had to know who was in my home.

I finally reached the large oak double doors. My shaking hand slowly grasped the handle before pushing it down to open it. I pushed open the door to the master bedroom slowly, hoping the noise of the floor was just the sound of the house settling though my gut told me otherwise. I turned the light on to see a man standing by the window. I gasped and jumped in fear, making him turn and look at me. He smiled a wicked smile that chilled me down to my very soul. I was sure I was done for, but as he came into the light, I knew him.

It was impossible. There was no way he could be standing there. He was the man who had haunted my dreams since I was a little girl.

Every night from the time I could first remember, he would come in my dreams. He was always kind and gentle with me, much like a sweet older brother.

As I grew, I began to see him more as a frightening desire than a sweet older brother. When I turned seventeen, I begged him to be real because I had fallen in love with him. He gave me one final kiss before leaving to make it a reality. It had been fifteen years since that night.

"Welcome home. I have waited so long for you," he revealed in a seductive voice that made me feel as if my knees would give out.

I clung to the door, frightened and trying to maintain my balance as my mind fought to make sense of this. He was stunningly handsome, more so than I remember. His jet-black hair was shorter and perfectly groomed, parted on one side. His olive skin was flawless and made each of his strong muscles look perfect under his button-down shirt. But, it was the eyes I remember the most, those blood-red eyes.

He smirked at me. "Do you remember me, Alyx? I promised you long ago we would be together. Remember? You begged for it."

He was there with me as a child. When I was five, I was sitting in my room playing with my dolls when I heard my floorboards creak from my closet. Curiously I got up and opened the door. I knew I was safe in my room, or at least that is what my mother taught me.

The darkness of my closet shrouded him for a moment before the light finally traveled up his body as if it was giving him life. A tall man, six-foot at least, stood there with his eyes closed. When the light finally finished illuminating him, he opened his eyes that glowed the deep blood-red hue they had in my dreams.

Oddly, I should have been scared, but I was more excited than anything. He was the man of my dreams who would take me to fun and exotic places.

"Sebastian! I didn't think you could visit?" I asked, perplexed.

He smiled a wicked smile before it grew soft and caring. He knelt at my level. "I couldn't until you wished for it. Now I am here to spend time with you." His voice was the most beautiful thing I had ever heard.

"Yay! Come play with me!" I said excitedly as I tried to take his hand, but my hand went through him as if he was made of air. Naturally, I tried again but had the same reaction. "Why can't I touch you?" I asked sadly.

"I am not of this world, my dear child. I can keep you company, but that is all," he replied in a tone as sad as mine.

"How will you play with me?"

"Let me show you." He said, sitting on the floor across from me and my toys. He lifted my toy bear with his finger making it float and move as if he were holding it. "Would you like to have a tea party?" he said in a silly gruff voice.

I giggled and held up my doll. "Why yes, Mr. Bear, I would," I said, pouring the imaginary tea into all the cups.

"Thank you. Such wonderful tea," he replied in the same silly gruff voice.

My door opened, and my mother looked in on me. "Hi,

honey…" She stopped looking straight at Mr. Bear floating above the floor for a few minutes before dropping to the floor.

"Hi, Mommy, we are playing tea party," I said, not realizing the problem.

"That's great, honey. Was your bear floating?" she asked nervously.

"No, that was Sebastian," I replied with childish innocence.

"Oh, who is Sebastian?"

"My friend."

"Best not tell her anymore, my dear. She wouldn't understand."

"Oh, okay," I replied to him.

"Honey, no one is in here with you."

"She can't see me. She isn't allowed to," he said to me.

"He is too."

"I am going to go call Dr. Garner."

Sebastian stood up. "This isn't good. If they give you medicine, don't take it. It will hurt you. Just give it to me." He said firmly and protectively.

Years later, Sebastian was still with me. Now when he would visit my dreams, I could feel him hold me and touch me. He was more like my protective big brother than a friend now. The more my parents tried to bring priests, pastors, and doctors around me, the more things would happen in the house.

People would get hurt. The chairs would move and break

on their own. Other times he would force them to stick to the ceiling. Things would go flying across the room toward people. Sometimes it would be papers or books to distract the person. Then other times, it would be glasses or knives, depending on what they tried to do to me.

At one point, a pastor said that the things happening were all from me and I should be committed to keep from hurting anyone else. That was the first night Sebastian growled and roared in anger.

"YOU. WILL. NOT. TOUCH. HER!" He roared, shaking the house walls as he pulled me behind him.

At that moment, I realized everyone else heard him too, as they all looked around in horror. The preacher crossed himself.

"Your god has no power over me!" Sebastian shouted again before flinging the preacher against the wall, breaking his collarbone.

For a while after that, my parents finally stopped having me tested and tried the tried-and-true method of denial. That was until my great-uncle came to visit.

Sebastian could now touch me, but I still couldn't touch him. I was still happy that his strength and adoration for me was growing. It would be false to say mine wasn't growing for him too.

That night when we sat at dinner, my uncle sat next to me. He said I was very grown up though I was only thirteen. It was nice to have someone who wasn't afraid of me or, rather, Sebastian.

Toward the end of dinner, I felt a hand on my knee moving up under my dress. Looking back over my shoulder, I saw Sebastian too far away to be touching me. I looked down to see it was my uncle's hand. When my heart began to race, Sebastian grabbed hold of my uncle, jerking him from the table. My uncle gripped my thigh hard and left deep scratches on my thigh. When his hand was pulled from my thigh, he grasped my dress, pulling it and ripping it as he was jerked away.

"What part of don't fucking touch her do you pathetic humans not understand?!" his voice boomed throughout the house.

"We haven't!" my father cried out in fear.

"You didn't. He did! Do you know what happens to child molesters in hell? We take our time with them!" he said as all the knives in the knife block flew at my uncle.

I watched as my uncle squirmed and whimpered, eventually peeing himself.

"We carve them up like fat Thanksgiving turkeys," he said as one knife carved down my uncle's body, cutting his shirt only. "We bleed them," he said, as two more knives quickly cut his shirt sleeve like they were slitting his wrists, but never cut him. "Then we gut them and play in their entrails," he said as the butcher knife cut open his pants and belt. This time the knife cut an 'X' right on his penis. "Now you are marked. So, the next time you even think about a child, you will feel that scar. You will know I and every demon haunting earth will watch you, ready to torment you. We get hungry and bored. We will make you our playground. Go and spend the rest of your days in guilt for what you were about to do to her! You will owe her before the end!" he said as his eyes became visible to my uncle. I could see them glow a terrifying red.

That was the only time I ever saw my great uncle until his attorney showed up telling me he had left me this estate.

When I turned seventeen, I fell so in love with him that it broke my heart. I was in a deep depression and even thought about suicide just to be with him. His touches and warm words of love always stopped me, but it grew to be too much.

"Don't you see what you are doing to me?" I shouted at him one afternoon.

"I do, but I can't become corporeal yet. Please don't hurt yourself. It is torment for me as well not to feel your touch, your kiss. All that keeps me strong is your love. Please wait for me?" he said as I saw black tears roll down his cheeks.

"It is killing me to keep waiting!" I cried too.

"I know. I know of one way that would be faster, but I must leave you for a time," he said as he cupped my face in his hands.

"How long? I can't live forever without you." I sobbed into his touch.

"I don't know, but I know you are strong. Wait for me, Alyx. I will return. I swear it as I have sworn to protect you," he told me firmly.

All I could do was nod; with that, he was gone.

For five long years, I was broken and became hollow without him. There would be times I would feel him, but I could never find him. I even thought I must have been insane, but the more I learned about psychology, the more I understood what he was couldn't happen.

When my great-uncle died, I wanted him close, but all I had were my memories. My memories of good, bad, terrifying moments, but all the moments of my demon.

My eyes slowly opened as memories flooded back into my mind, "Sebastian?" I whispered as he made his way to me.

He gave me a loving grin before he pulled me to him. His touch was his. His scent was his. He had returned.

My hands drifted up his chest as surprise coursed through me. "How?"

He smiled down at me. "I needed a soul of this world. I took your uncle's. I tormented him and built my strength for the last five years, and when he died, I took his power. Now I can be here with you. In this world and the next."

Emotions ran through me, but I did the only thing that felt right. I leaned up and kissed him passionately. The fires of Hell burned into me, and I felt whole for the first time in my life. He was my soul mate.

My arms slipped around his neck as my lips parted, inviting him in. He held me tight against his muscular frame as he kissed me with all the built-up passions of our years together and apart. For so long, he was the demon I had longed for, and at last, he was mine.

Return to Odin's Arms

The moonlight shone brightly through the trees
As they whipped past me.
The echoing unison of my paws
Falling against the earth as I ran,
And the pounding of my heart in my chest,
Drummed in my ears like the drums of war.
Though my paws knew these woods
Better than my eyes,
I knew I couldn't stop.
They had come for me.
Why? I may never truly know,
But the hourglass sands of life
Were nearing the final grain.
My only downfall besides the sounds of my breath
And my paws beating against the earth

Was the bright summer equinox moon
That lit my path through the woods.
Though the forest seemed silent,
I could hear the last grains of
The hourglass of my life falling
And the hoof beats of Death's stallion
Coming for me.
They were too close.
I quickly glanced around, trying to spot them,
Only to see no life
Just the eerie forest surrounding me.
I looked up at the moon,
Cursing her silently, only to feel
The painful thud in my back.
I could taste the bitter copper of my blood
As it began to flood into my mouth.
I looked at my side to see the blood
Coating my white fur around the silver arrow.
My eyes drifted back as I began to fall.
That's when I saw her, the Huntress.
She had called him, and Death had come.
My master and Valhalla now await.

The Tenant

The house was perfect for a single woman who had just come into the fruitful prime of her career. She had no attachments, no man, dog, or even fish. She found the adorable two-bedroom cottage on a property listing website and knew she had to have it. A few months later, the paperwork was finished, and the loan was secured. She was now the owner of the home. The closing document was the last thing that had to be signed.

It was a delightful and warm spring Tuesday evening when she arrived to sign the final document and begin her move. She saw her realtor standing at the front door waiting for her. She walked up to him and shook his hand.

"Ready to be the owner of your home?" he asked with his charismatic smile.

"I am. Shall we go inside and sign the papers?" she

answered, needing to finish the procedure and make her home her own.

He led her inside to the kitchen and got out the forms and keys to the house. He spread them out for her on the counters so she could sign all the marked lines. When she finished signing, he handed her the keys, quickly gathered the papers, and turned to the door.

"Before I go, I must tell you something. You need to meet the tenant who lives here as well. Meet him. Please. You are such a sweet girl, and I would hate to see something happen to you because you refused to introduce yourself to him. There is a door in the back of the closet in the master bedroom. Open it, and follow the stairs. You will find him there. He will introduce himself to you in a not-so-nice fashion if you don't do this. Please, my dear, do not wait." he said to her pleadingly before rapidly leaving, not giving her a chance to respond.

She looked at him, utterly perplexed, as she watched him leave. "Stairs? This is a single-level house," she questioned.

She walked through the house cautiously before she turned on the light in the master bedroom and walked to the closet. There was no way this could be true. She thought to herself as she walked to the back of the closet and found a door handle.

As she touched the door handle, a door shimmered into the light. The door was an ancient wooden door with markings and symbols she had never seen. She twisted the handle, and it squeaked as if it hadn't turned in centuries. She pulled open the door and saw an arrangement of wooden stairs built into the side of a brick wall. She looked out straight ahead and saw the opposite side was a dull and profound chasm of the void that gave her an ethereal vibe of being "alive."

She strolled up the stairs, feeling them groan under her step. Her hand ran along the damp brick wall to the top of a narrow platform that seemed to wrap and twist around like a labyrinth through the darkness. Off to the right of the narrow platform were doors of every shape and color, each showing signs of wear. In the middle of the labyrinth was a circular platform with three doors around it. It appeared not to be held up by anything, just simply coasting above the abyss. The strange room was dimly lit by baseball-sized balls of white, red, and purple fire that floated above.

She saw a man step out of the shadows when she finished taking in her surroundings. He was slender, dressed in an ornate three-piece suit, with his short black hair perfectly groomed and parted on the side. Each aspect made him more handsome than the one before until she saw his eyes. The deep black eyes told her he looked human, but he wasn't.

He gave her an alluring grin that made her go a little weak in her knees. "You must be the new tenant. I am Lucian," he said in a voice that was like velvet to her ears.

She nodded slowly as her heart pounded loudly in her chest. "I... I am. I am Katrina. I just bought the house. What are you, and how is this place possible?" she asked as she saw him hold out his hand to her.

"I won't bite. I just want to show you around my home," he told her, holding his hand out to her.

Against her better judgment, she gradually grasped his hand, which was so feverous. She looked down at his hand. "Can you…please answer my questions?" she asked him as her dread could be heard in her voice.

He began to lead her down the path. "This is *my* home. Your home simply happens to be a piece of it. I am a demon.

An incubus, to be particular. I won't ever hurt you unless you attempt to hurt me. We can live in peace. I only ask you to let me feed on you occasionally," he said as he led her down the path past many doors.

She was in shock at this point. "A demon…you need to feed on me, how?"

"Well, do you know what an incubus is?" he solicited, as one of the entryways opened, and a deafening thing was screaming on the other side. "Excuse me one moment, please? Just…don't move," he said to her as he walked through the entryway. Before long, a frightening snarl came from the other side, and a stream of fire shot out of the door.

She watched in horror, unable to look inside the door to see what was happening. Each sense inside her advised her to run, but she found herself unable to leave. Worry and fear for him crept inside her, driving her to stay.

A couple of long minutes later, he exited, rectifying his suit coat and vest. "I apologize about that. In addition to being an incubus, I am also a keeper of several realms. They are also my tenants. That was the furious spouse of one of my female benefactors. Are you married?" he asked, grasping her hand again and driving her up the way that appeared to develop more perilous as they strolled, for she no longer had the safety of the wall.

She held his hand tighter, afraid of falling. "I do know what an incubus is and no, I am not married," she said delicately.

He looked back at her. "No? No boyfriend either, I am speculating?" he said, stopping and looking her over.

She shook her head as she nearly kept running into him as he halted to look her over. "Uh…no. Why?" she asked, confounded.

He grinned once more. "Oh, nothing. It's just easy to tell," he said to her, leading her again down the path.

"Tell? How? And you never answered my other question. How will you feed?" she asked, wanting answers if this 'man' would be living with her.

He laughed a bit. "Well, I will feed off your sexual energy. I can tell you haven't had…it…in a while because your energy is deficient. I will feed on you when you are alone or with a lover, but the best way to feed on you is to be with you," he said, reaching the entry to a bridge that led to a platform in the center, but the boards of the bridge were missing as if they had fallen into the abyss.

With an influx of his hand, blocks flew from obscurity and started to fill in the missing bits of the bridge. He led her to that point, but her feet wouldn't take her across the new boards. "That isn't safe. We shouldn't cross that," she said, stepping back until his arm was extended.

"Have I given you a reason not to trust me? I assure you it is very safe." He said, hopping on the boards to demonstrate her. "Come with me, my Katrina. I have a surprise for you. It will show you that I am not doing all this to hurt you."

She took a tentative step onto the boards, and they held her weight as if they were stone. Lucian pulled her nearer to him as he drove her to the middle platform. She saw the boards fall into the chasm, yet she never heard them arrive at the bottom.

"Pick a door." He advised her as he relinquished her hand.

"Why?" she asked him mindfully.

"If I let you know, it will ruin the surprise. Just pick a door," he said with a sweet grin.

She looked at the doors, and finally picked the light green door that reminded her of spring. When she strolled through, she was met with delicate green lush earth. She was in the weeping willow grove she had known from her youth. It was a spring day when the sun demonstrated gleams of itself through the branches and weeping teardrop leaves. The grass was still not extremely tall but rather delicate and brimming with wildflowers. The delicate chatter of the creek still streamed with clear water that sparkled in the beams of the warm sun.

She smiled and laughed as she flopped down on the earthen bed, getting a charge out of the excellence and haven of the forest. "How is this possible?" she asked, shutting her eyes and getting a charge from the hints of the stream and songbirds in the trees.

"Some demons are insidious, and are in this world to bring loathing, decimation, and disarray. However, others, similar to me, are most certainly not. We bring seduction, love, and safety from a cruel world. Our magic is nothing but satisfaction if we choose it to be. If you make us angry, we bring madness, discord, and the pain of pleasure that nothing can cure. That is why Roger, your realtor, told you to introduce yourself to me. If you are good to me, I will be good in return. This is your sanctuary, Katrina. You will have access to it whenever you need it," he said to her as he sat beside her and pulled out a crystal carafe full of the most beautiful, amber-colored liquid she had ever seen.

"The catch, I have to give you pleasure whenever you want?" she said, sitting up.

"No, well yes, but no. It would be a pleasure you would want as well. I would never harm you," he said, handing her a wine glass of the liquid.

"And what if I say no? Will you then take it from me?" she asked, taking a sip of the liquid. It was cool and filled her mouth with the sensation of the taste of perfect honey, apples, and a hint of the spice of clove.

“No? No one has ever told me ‘No’ before. I would not force you if that is what you mean. You ache for affection and a partner to share your existence with, and I could give you that. I suppose you could say, I have been searching for that too.”

She took a gander at him, confounded. “A demon seeks companionship?” she asked in almost a satirical tone.

“You don’t think demons get lonely? Sex is just a means to an end, even to your kind, but companionship is the ideal goal, is it not?” His black eyes investigated her emerald eyes.

"Wouldn't most simply take it?” She felt as if they were playing a game of cat and mouse.

“Most would. Be that as it may, I am not most. If I seek feeding or sex, I can find it anywhere, but a human companion who could withstand the draw of my magic would be ideal. Most go mad at a glimpse of it. They can't withstand the draw of my desire, and they start to lose their grasp on reality.”

“You know that isn’t a selling point for you, don’t you?” she said with a giggle.

“I would have left that out for most, but you are so strong-willed. My magic barely seems to affect you. No decision is required now. Think about it. We can just be friends for now if you wish. Just consider my offer,” he said to her brushing his fingers against her cheek.

She nodded and finished her wine. “I should be getting back. I have a lot of unpacking left to do,” she said softly to him, but some of her enjoyed his touch.

“I will take you back, but your unpacking is done. I dipped into your mind momentarily to see how you would want it.

It's all done and set up for you." The wine and basket disappeared with a wave of his hand.

He stood and grasped her hand, helping her up. Then led her through the door again back onto the platform.

"You were in my head?!" she said, just acknowledging what he said to her.

He chuckled. "Only long enough to see what you wanted to do with the house. If you don't like it, I will correct it for you. Consider this my first act as a possible companion," he said, still chuckling.

He led her to the bridge. There wasn't a need to call for the boards this time. He led her back down the winding platform path.

"What is down there? Does it even have a bottom?" she asked, gazing down into the chasm.

He stopped quickly and turned her face away. "Never stare! There are things down there that are not nearly as kind as I am! They will stop at nothing to get to you if you draw attention to yourself by staring! I will keep you safe here, but never come without me. Do you understand me, Katrina?" He advised her sternly, yet his touch was delicate and protective.

She nodded slowly as she looked up into his eyes. "I understand. How will I reach you or the sanctuary if I can't come alone?" she said to him.

"Call for me. Simply say my name, and I will come to you," he advised her as his thumb stroked her cheek.

"Anytime?" she asked softly.

"Anytime," he said to her intimately.

He led her back down the pathway, past the doors, back down the stairs to hers. As he walked through with her into the now full closet, and as the door closed to his home, she felt as if they were being watched.

The bedroom was perfect. Artwork hung on the walls, her bed was made with her dark purple orchid bed set, and the delicate sparkle of candles glimmered on the end tables.

"You got this all correct. Thank you," she said with a soft blush, grateful for his magic.

"You are most welcome, my dear," he whispered in her ear as he ran his hands down her arms.

She closed her eyes and enjoyed his touch for a moment as she allowed her mind to wander, imagining what it might be like with him. Images of passion and love filled her mind until her eyes opened, and they were as black as his.

She gasped and stepped away from him. "Did you do that?" she asked, frightened.

He nodded. "I only nudged them in the direction they could go. Nothing more," he told her with a playful grin.

"Don't do that! If we are to be friends, stay out of my head! And why were my eyes black like yours?" she said, confronting him furiously.

He removed his suit coat and laid it over the foot of her bed. "It was an offer. On the off chance that we are to be as one, you will age and die. I will not. You could become a demon, like me, or a demon that will suit your soul and be mine forever. I meant no offense. Like I said, it was only an offer..."

"What makes you think I would want that? Maybe you should go. I think I have had enough excitement for one day." She let him know that she was still irate with him.

"Have a good night, then. If you wish me to stay out of your mind, I will. Sleep well, my Katrina," Lucian told her before grabbing his suit jacket and heading back through her closet.

She heard the door close. She sighed and scoffed as she shook her head and began to get ready for bed.

It had been weeks since she met Lucian, but she couldn't force herself to visit him again, regardless of her sentiments of missing him. He kept his distance until she was ready to see him though he also missed her. It was a connection they were both unfamiliar with.

Her dreams were a haunting form of torture for them both. Dreams that made him insane with longing. A desire he could quench by force, but he wanted her to love him as he was beginning to love her.

He couldn't take much more and decided he had to see her, but she wasn't at home when he walked through the door. He could tell she hadn't been for a few days.

"Katrina… where are you? I need you," he groaned.

He was too weak from staving off feeding until she was ready for him. His lack of feeding made his power to track her feeble.

He walked back through the door, looked up at her three doors, and let out a deafening demonic roar. He had never fallen for anyone the way he had fallen for her. The yearning and desire for her was devouring him from the inside out.

His mind raced with thoughts of her with another. "Katrina! Can't you hear me screaming for you?" He thundered again, causing his inhabitants to look in on him. "You are the only one who can save me from hell…my hell." He cried out as if she could hear him.

He walked past the cracked doors and prying eyes as if he

was a broken man. He made his way up to her platform. The sanctuary he had gifted her.

Long claws protruded from his fingertips. "Where are you? Have you left me?" His hunger pushed him to a place where his thoughts of the unknown consumed him. "No one can save me from this pain," he said, growling before slashing his claws at the green door, leaving deep marks in the wooden door.

He looked at the claw marks and growled at himself. He needed to be free from his pain and the desires that boiled within him. He ran off the platform, jumping into the black abyss, letting it consume him.

Katrina woke from a dead sleep in her hotel room in Chicago. She was attending a conference for work, but her heart pounded in her chest, and her gut twisted with the overwhelming sensation something was wrong. Terribly wrong. She couldn't stand the inclination inside her.

She dressed, packed her things, and called her boss on the way to her car but hung up before he could answer. There was no way she couldn't explain this to him. He wouldn't understand. She was coming home tomorrow, but something told her she couldn't wait.

Three hours later, she walked in her front door. Her panic in her gut grew as she walked towards her bedroom. The entrance to the abyss was cracked open.

"Lucian…Oh god…" She rushed to the entryway and pulled it open.

She looked out into the void before whispering. "Lucian?

Are you alright?" Her dread of this place filled her without him there to protect her.

As she spoke, she looked out and saw a pair of red eyes looking at her from the darkness. Screaming, she stumbled back into her closet and kicked the door closed. She cowered in the corner, trying to become one with the shadow. She hoped hiding would keep her safe from the fear that whatever peered at her from the shadows would come for her.

A few minutes later, the door burst open, and a figure ran past her.

"Katrina!" Lucian called, rushing through the house and searching for her.

"Lucian…" She called from her hiding spot.

"I was so afraid somet… why are you hiding?" he said, kneeling in front of her. "What happened?"

He looked terrible. He was a disheveled mess. His typically flawless attire was torn, dirty, and bloody. He even looked sickly.

The worry now mixed with her fear, "Something saw me. These red eyes were just staring at me…I was afraid it was going to come after me," she said, shaking.

He closed the door and wrapped his arms around her delicately. "Nothing will come for you. They wouldn't try something that inept."

"What happened to you while I was gone? You…you look terrible," she asked as her fear began to ease in his arms.

"It's nothing. I just haven't fed in a few weeks. What is more important is you are safe."

She pushed away from him a bit. "Lucian, why haven't you fed?" she asked, clearly worried.

"Another time, I promise. You should rest. You are exhausted."

She looked at him, confused. "How did you…never mind. You're right," she said, standing up.

He wanted to carry her to bed, but he couldn't. He tucked a piece of her hair behind her ear. "Rest well, my Katrina," he said before kissing her forehead and turning to leave her.

"Stay close. Please?" she asked him softly.

"Always," he answered with a tender grin.

She went and changed in her bathroom before crawling into her bed. She watched him look at her longingly before disappearing through the door.

She stared up at the ceiling, wondering if he had disappeared behind that door. Little did she know he was sitting against the door. It was easier for him to be close to her.

She couldn't stop thinking about how he looked. It worried her. *Just this once.* She thought to herself as she slowly slipped her hand down her body and began running it over her sex. She closed her eyes as she let her fingers follow her fantasy.

Usually, her fantasies involved a sexy character from a book or movie or just a handsome man, but as of late, they were of Lucian. She had disregarded them because she didn't want to give the idea that she had feelings for a demon, but they both needed those fantasies now.

She dipped her fingers into her panties and bit her lip, imagining he was kissing her body as he touched her.

As a soft moan escaped her lips, he felt her sexual energy. He closed his eyes and breathed the delectable aroma in his nose. He stood up and rested his forehead against the door as he opened his mouth, and the red rose-colored vitality wafted into his mouth.

Her fingers ran over her folds teasingly before slipping the tip of her middle finger inside of her. She was astonished to find how aroused she was near Lucian.

Thoughts of his hungry hands wandering and groping her flesh filled her mind. Aching kisses with gentle nibbles placed on her neck and shoulders. She could feel his endowed manhood pressing against her thigh as his fingers slipped inside her and curled up to her g-spot.

A gasp and a louder moan escaped her lips as she slipped her middle and ring fingers inside her depths and began to pulse them in and out of her slowly.

"Lucian…" she moaned, barely above a whisper.

He growled as his claws protruded from his fingertips, again digging into the door that separated them as he savored her longing and desire.

"Call me again, and I will come to you…Call to me Katrina." He snarled back in the desire for her.

Her body began to feel his manhood slipping inside her, slowly making her body ache for him. Her fingers slipped in and out of her wetness faster. Her moans carried through the bedroom and into his ears like sweet music.

His demon ears could hear the sounds her fingers made with every plunge into her sweet sex. Each thrust and moan made him stronger as he drank in her succulent sexual energy.

Katrina moaned louder as her fantasy consumed her, making her climax build quickly. "Oh god…yes! Fuck me!" she cried out.

He let out another growl as he fought his urge to go to her and claim her as his. He slammed his fist into the brick, causing it to crack and crumble. His claws raked down, leaving deep grooves in the brick. "Damn it, Katrina, I need you. Call to me!" he growled.

She screamed out in pleasure as she climaxed, feeling his

energy. When she came down, she got up and headed to her bathroom to clean up before heading back to bed to sleep.

She never called him, but she hoped what she gave him was enough.

The next few days, she was tormented by the memories of that night, and she decided she needed just to try a date with an ordinary man. After work, she headed to one of the local bars and began to flirt with the nearest handsome guy she could find. She needed to just let herself go with a stranger.

Later that night, she walked into the house with a handsome man in a leather jacket. He was tall, with a tanned complexion and profound chestnut eyes. His goatee and a scar on his left eyebrow gave him a bad-boy appeal that was very attractive to her.

"Can I get you a glass of wine or something?" she said to him as he glanced around.

"No thanks, doll. I think I would enjoy something more delicious, and with those long legs, I could drink you in for days," he told her, shamelessly flirting with her as he wrapped his arms around her waist, pulling her against him.

She giggled and enjoyed the feeling of his firm body against hers, but before she could tell him to slow down, his lips were already on her neck.

He whispered in her ear, "Which way to your bedroom?"

She smiled and took his hand, and led him to her bedroom. "Give me just a minute, please?" she told him before heading off to the bathroom.

He sighed as he took off his jacket. "Don't take too

long…" he said so she could hear him. "I would hate for you to miss your appointment with death." He said to himself with a shrewd grin as his eyes flashed a dark red shade.

Lucian had waited for her to call to him, but she hadn't. He didn't want to push since he had been searching lifetimes for her and knew she was the one he needed. He listened day in and day out to make sure she was safe, but tonight something felt wrong.

When she returned home, he heard another voice with her. A voice that was not human. He made his way through one of the doorways and down through the labyrinth. Each step he took made his dark heart pound in fear for her, forcing his feet to carry him faster.

Katrina took off her heels before exiting the bathroom. "Now, where were we?" she asked as the door inside her closet burst open.

She let out a short scream as Lucian burst in, he was not in the suit she had last seen him in, but in a white dress shirt, black suspenders, and black slacks; his eyes met hers with that deep blackness she had missed. He let out a deep growl as the other man stood and faced him.

She looked at him, "Lucian! What are you doing here?" she shouted, angry at him for bursting in.

He never looked at her; he only kept his eyes on her date. "Katrina…go to the sanctuary. Now please," he told her calmly.

"No…not until you tell me what the hell is happening!"

she told him sternly, but deep down, she knew something was wrong.

"Of all the times you must be defiant, please listen to me!" he contended.

"Maybe you should listen to him. After all, you did bring home a demon," her date told her as he looked at her with blood-red and glowing eyes.

"A demon? What do I have, a demon beacon or something on me?" she said, stepping closer to Lucian as her fear began to show.

"You do, my dear. Me. I established my connection with you when we met, which has grown since that night. It made others curious about you. I just never thought any of them would be stupid enough to come after you. He is a death demon. He feeds by killing. He planned to kill you the moment he got you under him in bed," Lucian said to her, holding out a hand to her.

Katrina took his hand, knowing Lucian had no reason to lie to her. She felt him pull her behind him. "Why do they want me?" She could feel fear begin to overcome her.

"Stupid human! We want you because your beautiful energies are the most delicious in all the realms, and your desire for him that you keep fighting has the most lustful aroma," the death demon told her with a cackle that sent a chill down her spine.

"Listen to me. Run to the sanctuary. It will open for you. It is the only place where you will be safe. Go, Katrina!" Lucian commanded her before shoving her back toward the door in the closet.

She felt him let go as she saw her date begin to transform from a human. As his tan skin changed to thick black scales and long claws grew from his fingers, she turned quickly and ran to the door. She didn't want to stay to see what he would become.

As she rushed up the stairs, she stopped at the top, hearing a strange noise in the usually eerily quiet place. She didn't want to look into the black abyss, but she glanced at it as she began to hear quick scratching, which was getting louder. She began to run again along the path as she reached the door that once had the loud screaming from it fly open.

A deep red dragon's head about three times the size of hers poked around the corner. "What in hellfire…oh no! Sweet child, you must run! Lucian will have a place that is safe for you. Go before they reach it!" she told her, stepping back so she could pass on the narrow path.

"A dragon?! You're a dragon! What the hell?" she started, but the dragon interrupted her.

"No time. Get to safety. You are the one he has told us about. You must go so he can fight them off!" She nudged her up the path.

As she stumbled, she saw a black shadow-like creature climb up on the path near the stairs to her home. She screamed and ran as fast as she could to the bridge. As she approached the bridge, the boards began to fly up and form the bridge again. She stepped on them as soon as they connected until she reached the center. She ran to the green door again, but as she opened it, her ankle was grabbed by another black shadow creature. The creature's grasp blazed like acid on her skin. She immediately kicked free and kept running into the sanctuary slamming the door behind her.

She collapsed by the brook and gradually plunged her ankle into the cool water as it sizzled and released steam. She cried and screamed in pain as the cool water cleaned and began to close her wound.

It felt like hours since she had barely gotten away, but there was still no sign of him until she heard a loud thunderous crash.

She got up quickly and slowly opened the door, afraid the creature might be lurking outside the door. As she did, she heard a loud booming roar.

"Listen up!" She heard Lucian shout into the abyss as she walked onto the center platform.

She could finally see him. He was covered in a black gooey substance, his clothes were ripped, and he was holding one of the shadow demons up by the throat.

"That woman, look at her, you worthless pieces of shit! See her? She is mine! No one will lay a claw on her ever again! I have killed many of you tonight, and if I must, I will kill every last one of you until she is safe! Am I fucking clear!?!" He shouted as his voice shook down the walls of the chasm.

He then snapped the neck of the shadow demon and tossed him to the hell below. Then he cracked his neck and slowly walked up the winding platform and crossed the bridge to get to her.

He ran his fingers down her arm. "One of them grabbed you. I can smell the burned flesh on you. Where are you hurt?" he asked with concern, but a flash of anger graced his face.

"It's healed, I think. I cleaned the wound in the water of the brook. Still aches, but not like before," she replied quietly as she stepped closer to him.

"You will have a scar that will ache and never fully heal."

"Oh…are you hurt?" she asked as her fingers ran over the tears in his shirt before slipping around his body slowly.

He smirked. "Not in a physical sense, but you could say I have some aches. I…burned for you."

She met his black eyes. "What do you mean?"

He let out a sigh, then turned her tenderly and demonstrated to her the profound claw marks in the red door. "I didn't feed because I wanted to feed on you. My connection to you grew strong, even apart. It was horrible to be away from you. I, at long last broke my promise and came to see you. You were gone. The demon in me that was starving and aching for you, I lost control. To keep the others safe, I dropped down into the bottom of the abyss. The tar pits welcomed me with open arms. I was convinced of repulsive things…I let them burn me…but then you called to me. I found strength I never knew. You were the healer, my angel in this darkness. I broke free and came to you."

She walked over and ran her fingers over the claw marks in the door. She then looked around and saw the grooves in the brick down by the door to her home. She turned back to him. "Were those from the same time too?"

"No. Those were from the night you pleasured yourself. I was fighting against my promise again. I wanted to go to you and give you the pleasure you were so desiring. I was waiting for you to call for me, you did that once, but when I looked into your mind and saw what you were fantasizing about, I waited to see if you would call me again. You didn't. So I fought my urge," he explained to her, gradually closing the distance between them. "I still ache for you," he said, as his hand gently caressed her cheek.

She blushed. "I see. I don't think it would be in the best interest of our health to deny our aches. Would it?" she asked coyly.

"Not at all. Our aches?"

"I have been fighting how I feel for weeks. I ache for you too, Lucian."

He let out a low growl and pressed her against the red door. "Say it. Tell me what you want, Katrina?"

She licked her lips as her eyes met the darkness in his. "I want you, Lucian. I need you. I am calling to you."

His lips pressed to hers, kissing her with the passions of all hellfire. His hand caressed her waist, pulling her against him. He needed to claim her as his. He broke the kiss before taking her hand and leading her through the red door.

Once she walked in, it was a beautiful, ornate bedroom with a king-size bed adorned with red and black silk sheets.

"Your home away from home." He told her as his arms slipped around her waist, pulling her close against him.

She smiled and pulled him down to her as she pressed her lips to his again. His lips were hot to the touch, like the rest of him, but soft like velvet against hers. The kiss continued taking them to a place where time nor the outside world could affect them.

The candles that dimly lit the room slowly extinguished themselves, and the door locked with a wave of his hand. This place and time was only for them.

Through the span of numerous months, Katrina's affection for Lucian developed and bloomed into what they had both been seeking. She rarely spent time in her home. Most of her time consisted of getting to know her love that had lived thousands of lifetimes.

One fateful night she woke from a nightmare in his arms, remembering the red eyes and the shadow demon that had tried to capture her. She clung to him tightly. He was her savior and her world, but each day that passed with him, she knew their love was limited while she was still human.

He held her tight, comforting her, swearing nothing would touch or harm her, but he knew deep down they would try again. It was only a matter of time until they came for her again.

She sat up in her bed, "I can't do this. I need to know I will be safe. You promise, but we both know that isn't exactly true. You can't guarantee they won't come for me, can you?"

Lucian also sat up. "No, I can't. There is only one surefire way they will lose interest in you. You would have to become a demon. None of them are interested in our kind unless there is something to fight over, like when that death demon came for you. They tried to kill me because they wanted you. They won't want you any longer if you become a demon. I promised you I wouldn't pressure you to do anything. I will love you forever, Katrina. Whether you say by side or eventually pass into the realms of the dead in my arms, I will love you," he explained, holding her hand as they sat together on the bed.

She looked at him, trying not to cry as she thought about leaving him. "I can't leave you. I won't. I want eternity with you."

Lucian looked at her and nodded. "Then come with me," he said, getting out of bed, taking her hand, and helping her stand.

He led her through the closet into his world and up the path, but instead of turning to take the bridge to her sanctuary, he continued deeper into the abyss.

Out of the corners of her eyes, she could see the shadows moving as if they were following them. "Lucian…the shadows…" she whispered.

"I know. We are almost there," he said, pointing to a large metal gate.

"What is in there?" she asked, clinging to him tighter.

With a wave of his hand, the gate began to rise. "Your future."

She looked at him nervously as they passed under the gate. She heard claws scratching behind them. As she turned to look, she saw claws trying to reach under the gate for her. She gasped and rushed ahead of Lucian.

"It's all right, child. They won't get you." A female voice said from all around her.

She held tight to Lucian, looking around before seeing a woman step out of a purple light.

"Hello, Mother," Lucian said with a soft smile.

"My son, it has been centuries," the beautiful woman said to him.

The voice was soothing to her ears, much like Lucian's, but she felt safe, as if she was a child in her mother's presence.

"You must be Katrina. My name is Lilith. I am a mother of demons. I do not create them. I change them. I heard your plea to become like us. Come with me, child. Lucian cannot go with you. Only you can take the path into the next life."

Katrina turned back to Lucian. "Will I be safe?" she asked more to Lilith than Lucian.

"Will you come out the other side still belonging to him? Yes. Safe is a relative term. Your human side must be given to the darkness so you can become like us," Lilith explained warmly.

"Go, I will be here when you return," he said before kissing her with such passion it even made Lilith surprised.

She blushed when he kissed her but returned the kiss,

clinging to him for a moment before slowly letting him go. "I love you." She said before walking with Lilith into the shadows.

"I love you too," he said to her as he watched her disappear.

Lilith led her for a long while before they walked into a clearing with a beautiful grove of scarlet red trees with black trunks. "This is the grove of creation," she explained to Katrina.

"Will it hurt?" Katrina asked, obviously scared.

"Only for a moment," she replied as they finally reached a pool of what looked like blood.

"Is that…blood?"

"You are born of blood as a human. You are reborn as a demon from the blood. Come now, step into the pool."

She walked over to the pool and stepped down into the thick liquid. When she reached the center, hands snaked up and began to reach up and pull her under. She tried to scream, but one of the hands clasped over her mouth. She was submerged for several long minutes before being pushed back to the top. Not a drop of blood remained on her. Her eyes remained closed until she stood on top of the pool.

Lilith smiled. "Welcome to our world, my dear."

As she heard Lilith speak, her eyes shot open and shined a brilliant purple. She strolled on top of the pool before venturing down before Lilith.

"I have known about your kind yet never met one up to this point. More often than not, the creation pool gives us incubi or succubi, or death demons. Never a Keeper." She paused for a moment. "Lucian and your world await," she said, pointing in the direction back to Lucian.

She could now see in the shadows. It was decorated much

like an old castle, and the pathways to the abyss were like the top floor of a glass skyscraper. The shadow demons were still there, yet now overlooked her.

Lucian saw her and smiled before picking her up to take her to their home through the black door of her platform. Though she had never been through the black door. She now realized this was the home she would share with him.

Three months later, her world had changed, and now sitting by the brook with her feet in the cool water, she wondered what the future would hold.

"How are you feeling, my dear?" Lucian asked as he sat next to her and held her hand.

"It's odd. I should feel different. However, I truly don't. Just happy and loved. A desire to protect is strong, very strong."

He chuckled and slipped his hand over her growing belly. "That is called motherhood, I believe. It also comes with your rank."

She ran her hand over his. "Which you have never explained to me?"

"You are a keeper of the offspring of damnation. They will come to you for direction, bearing, and obviously for requests as they develop, then they will go off into the domains and earn other titles." He replied as his hand slipped up between her breasts to her neck.

"Will it begin with our own?" she said as she wrapped her arms around him, holding him close.

"It will. We have eternity together now," he said as he

kissed and nipped her neck.

She shut her eyes in joy as she let his words simmer for a while. It was strange to think that death would never come for her now, but it was also liberating.

Her eyes glowed brilliant purple as she held him close and felt their child move within her.

Pocket Full of Wolfsbane

The cold moon of December was now just over the trees at the horizon, calling all the wild ones to venture out in its light. The clouds from the day's earlier snowstorm had finally moved out of the sky. A soft wind blew through the trees, spraying up some of the crystals of snow into the moonlight, making them glimmer. A large white wolf padded slowly through the forest, taking in the world before him.

Zaiden, one of the last large white werewolves left in this part of the world, was not going to ignore that call. As his paws felt the fresh powdery snow move and spread beneath his weight, he lifted his nose into the air. The icy air drifted into his lungs as he took in the scents of the world.

The smell of wolfsbane wafted on the night air. It was a smell he loved, despite the legends. He followed the scent through the shadows of the woods surrounding the graveyard. The mixture of valerian, nightshade, and death was usually enough to keep him away, but the herb intoxicated and urged him forward. Each step he took was muffled as the snow drifted between the toes of his paws. The world was quiet under a blanket of winter snow, and not much disturbed that silence. Only one sound pierced the veil of the forest tonight. The sound of soft humming drifted into his ears. The little girl's voice in the night made him stop and search for her.

Hidden in the shadows of the forest's edge, his eyes scanned over the expanse of the gravestones that sprawled out before him in search of the child. The broken-down cobblestone wall was once there to keep ones like him away from the sacred ground. The snow cover graves had little interest to him, only the scent of wolfsbane and the sweet little melody brought him here.

As his keen eyes combed over this land of the dead, he saw something move. Not far from him, he caught a glimpse of a little girl resting on the steps of an old mausoleum petting a small black kitten. The kitten pawed at the scarf tucked around her neck playfully. With her coat buttoned up tight, and her hood pulled up, hiding part of her face from his eyes, she looked almost at home. Though he knew a cold night with the graveyard lit by the full moon was no place for this little angel. As his eyes searched, he realized she was here alone. Laying silently in the shadows, he watched her play with her little furry friend by the moon's light.

A small bottle of rosemary and wild rose petals hung from her neck with a black obsidian orb chained to the bottle. He knew it was meant to protect her from evil, surrounding her with love, and keep luck on her side. He could finally isolate where the wolfsbane was coming from. The white strings of a small satchel stuck out of her pocket and wafted in the chilling wind. *A satchel in her pocket full of it, of course, to protect her from werewolves like him.* He smiled, knowing that it was a myth, wolfsbane to werewolves was much like catnip to cats. Only one race still enforced the old ways, witches, and he knew she was a daughter of a witch.

His ears twitched as he heard a voice on the cold winter night winds drifting through the graveyard like a siren's call.

"Maddie…Maddie, love, time to go!" the voice cried out to her.

"Come on, Lynx. It's time to go home," the little girl said, scooping up the kitten and tucking it into her coat.

Maddie. What a beautiful name, surely for a beautiful little witch. Zaiden thought to himself.

To his surprise, as the thoughts disappeared from his mind, the little girl turned and looked straight in his direction. She lifted her hood as her emerald eyes met his silver ones. Her delicate finger went to her lips as if she was telling him to keep a secret.

There was something about her eyes that enchanted him. He had never felt so compelled to protect someone in all of his two hundred and thirty-four years on this earth.

He followed after her in the shadows, keeping hidden from prying eyes. Stalking after her as if he were hunting, but he had no desire to hunt her. He only longed to know her.

He heard a soft giggle escape her lips as she looked back at him. He held off a bit as he listened to her mother call her again. Soon she stood in the light of a little cobblestone cottage on the outskirts of the city. A candle flickered in the window to light her way home. As she opened the door, she turned and waved at him before closing the door, forcing them to be parted.

Goodnight, sweet Maddie. I hope we meet again. He thought as he turned to leave her home before running into the woods for his full moon hunt.

Four Years Later

The warm summer breeze tousled strands of his hair away from his olive forehead. He ran his fingers through the strands pushing them away as he stepped from the woods surrounding the graveyard. Since that winter night, this had become one of his favorite places, but he had yet to come across that little angel again. The warm sun brushed over his skin from the patches shining through the trees. His fingers parted the tendrils of a weeping willow as he passed underneath its expansive canopy. He sat down against the trunk and closed his eyes to nap as the sounds of the quiet space of death filled his ears.

As quickly as sleep came to him, it fled with the sounds of footsteps and laughter. The laughter fluttered into his ears like the brush of a cool breeze on a hot day. His eyes opened and turned in the direction of the sound. He knew that laughter. It was her.

Maddie rushed through the graveyard, skipping and jumping over gravestones. This was still her favorite playground, and why shouldn't it be? A witch should feel at home amongst the dead. She stopped, feeling the presence of an old friend from long ago. She felt a smile grace her face as she looked in his direction. Her connection to him had grown since they had last seen each other, and so had her curiosity. She was no longer a timid little girl.

Hearing the call of her companions, she called back, never looking away from him. "Go on without me. I need to see someone first."

Her emerald eyes sparkled in the soft summer sun as the tall man emerged from the willow curtain. His dark brown hair was perfectly pushed back atop his head, his stoic olive face was enhanced by the dark brown stubble beard, and his well-built frame made her long for a hug from him, but she remembered those silver eyes the most. The eyes that had filled her with delight the first time she saw them in the shadows.

Zaiden walked towards her giving her a gentle smirk. She was not the little girl anymore. She now stood at the base of his chest. She was becoming an enchanting young lady. Her long blood-red hair laid softly on her shoulders as a few strands wafted in the wind, blowing across her porcelain ivory face. She still wore the same necklace as she did that night and still carried a satchel of wolfsbane in her pocket.

"I like this form too," she finally said, breaking the silence between them.

"It is much different from my wolf. Do you always play in graveyards?" he asked gently as the smell of the wolfsbane filled his nose.

"Yes. I love being near the dead. They make good company for a witch, or at least that is what my mother has always said. Do you always lurk in graveyards?" she asked playfully.

"Only when little witches play with pockets full of wolfsbane," he retorted, crouching down to be closer to her level.

"Well, it's to keep werewolves away, but I think that may be wrong since you are here," she blushed sweetly.

"Well then, may I tell you a secret?" a playful glint passed over his eyes.

"Of course, you can. I love secrets. Witches keep the secrets of the past, present, and future," she told him proudly.

He laughed, "That they do. Wolfsbane will not repel werewolves. It is actually an attractant to us. To repel a werewolf, incense of mugwort and witch's grass works much better, though I hope you will never use that against me," he told her gently.

"I would never use that against someone who has been so kind to me," she said, returning and hearing her friends' call again. "I like when you are near. I always hoped I would see you again."

He felt a tug at his heart as he renewed his vow to himself to protect her as long as she would let him. "Listen closely, not all are as kind as I, Maddie. You must be very careful. I will protect you when I can, but I can't always stay close. Our kinds do not always mix."

"I know…hey, you know my name! Now, that is not fair. You know my name, but I don't know yours," she said, almost pouting.

He chuckled at her innocence, "I am Zaiden. We seem to have a connection. Simply call my name if you ever need me. I will come as quickly as I can, but your friends are coming back looking for you, so I should go. Be safe, little angel," he said, winking at her before turning to leave her.

"Zaiden? When can I see you again? I'd rather we not wait another four years," she asked him to make him stop. He turned back to her, "I will return here to the willow tomorrow." He replied before disappearing into the woods before her friends could see him.

The next day, when Zaiden woke, he looked out his cabin window and saw it was pouring rain. This would not usually bother him, but he did worry about young Maddie. He cooked up some breakfast for himself before venturing out in the cool summer rain. His cabin was only a few miles from the graveyard, but it was probably best that he didn't show up naked after venturing there in wolf form.

It would take him about an hour to make his way to the graveyard, where he promised to meet her. On his way, he cut some wild lilies for her. The deep red and yellow flowers reminded him of her red hair. He had heard legends of how witches would entrance his kind to make them their slaves, but he wondered if those were myths like those of wolfsbane.

Once he stepped under the willow canopy, he received a bit of shelter from the downpour. He shook some of the water off of him as he waited. It wasn't long until he could feel her presence.

Maddie ran out into the rain as quickly as her feet could carry her. He came to her. She knew it. Perhaps it was a witch trait, but it was something she couldn't explain. She just wanted to see him again.

She ran under the canopy and rushed to him, hugging him. She then pulled back quickly and blushed.

Zaiden was stunned by the hug, but as he hugged her back, she pulled away quickly. "What's wrong, little lass?"

"I didn't know if you would like a hug. I only followed what felt right," Maddie replied, still blushing.

He laughed and opened his arms, "I like hugs."

She hugged him again with a smile. He felt like a big brother she would never have. She clung to him until he slowly started to let her go.

He picked up the bundle of flowers and handed them to her. "I picked them on the way."

They sat under the canopy of the willow, talking and learning about each other until the sun began to set. She didn't want the day to end, but the sun must set so the night can have its turn to shine.

"Your mother will be expecting you soon," he said softly as he stood, then helped her stand.

"I know. Will I see you again soon?" she asked softly.

"Call for me, and I will come."

She smiled and hugged him before picking up the bouquet and waving goodbye to him as she headed home.

Over the next few years, Zaiden would wander into the graveyard, and she would come running to find him. He had become the big brother and best friend she never had before. Under the summer sun lounging under the canopy of the willow, or walking and talking on the eerie fall days, they always seemed to find time for each other.

On her sixteenth birthday, she rushed out of the house after having an argument with her mother. The graveyard was always her sanctuary because no one would dare disturb her. No one except Zaiden.

The graveyard was cold this fall. It would be a long winter if it was this cold in September. She pulled her coat tight around her and pulled up her hood. She wiped a tear away. As the memory of the fight replayed freshly in her mind.

"Don't you understand that you will one day take my place in the coven? You need to get your head out of your daydreams!" her mother

shouted to her.

"Who said I even wanted to take your place? Maybe I want a solitary path! But you never stop running to see that or see me!" Maddie shouted.

"Oh, child, you don't even know what I am protecting us from! A solitary path would be fine, but you must learn the craft first! You spend all your days daydreaming in that damn graveyard. The dead can't will your future!"

"For a witch who can read the future, you are quite blind! You don't know anything about me!" Maddie shouted as tears welled in her eyes and she stormed out of the house.

"Maddie! Maddie!" her mother shouted before the door slammed.

Maddie dipped under the shelter of the tendrils of the willow she and Zaiden had come to call their own. She slumped down against the trunk, letting the skirt of her dress pool around her like the black abyss of emptiness she was feeling.

She stared at the long blade-like leaves on the ground as they began to lift and dance in the air. As her emotions shifted back and forth from emptiness to sadness to anger, the leaves danced violently until she heard a sound, and all of them became earthen daggers flying in the direction of the sound.

Zaiden quickly ducked and lunged to the side, avoiding all but one that had sliced his arm.

He looked over at Maddie. "Good Gods, Maddie! What did I do for you to want to harm me?" he said, holding out his hands in defense.

Her gaze was broken at the sound of his voice. She saw the blood dripping down his arm. She rushed over to him and hugged him tightly. "I am sorry! I never meant to hurt you. I…I had a fight with my mother. I walked out on her…" She said, crying against his muscular chest.

He wrapped his arms around her. "It's all right, my little witch. You're getting more talented. I will have to do something to announce when I am close; otherwise, it might be dangerous," he said, chuckling. "What was the fight about?"

"My future," she said as she clung tighter to him, letting the sound of his heart soothe her fears and anger.

"Ah, I see. What was she asking for?" he asked as he gently let her sit in the tree's shelter.

She sat beside him and laid her head on his strong shoulder. "She wants me to learn more about the craft and have a more active role in the coven. I prefer to be alone…well, with you."

Zaiden smiled softly, "I prefer that too, but just as I must hunt, you need to learn your craft. Learn what the coven has to offer, and when you come of age, you can make your choice. I will be here to support you."

"You agree with her?" she said, a bit shocked, and looked at him.

"To an extent. My little witch, you have much to learn, and I cannot teach it to you, but your coven and mother can. All you have to do is let them."

"It would mean I would see you less. I don't want that."

"I understand. We will make time as we always have."

He waited for her by the willow on the cold winter night of her twentieth birthday, but she was late. If there was one thing Maddie never was, it was late, not when he was coming to meet her. Worry filled him, but so did thoughts of doubt. *Perhaps my little witch has outgrown me.*

As the moon began to rise, he could feel his wolf aching to be released from his internal cage. He would have to leave, despite his longing to stay.

He tucked the gift inside a hollow knot in the tree, knowing she would find it before he left to prepare for his full moon hunt.

An hour later, she came running into the graveyard with her cat Lynx not far behind her. She had grown into an enchanting woman. Her blood-red hair was now long and flowed down past her mid-back. Her porcelain skin remained unchanged, as when she was a child, and she now stood up as tall as his chin. It was most noticeable when she hugged him. She often told him how she fit so perfectly against him.

She looked around for him but didn't see him. She internally damned herself, not realizing exactly how late she was from her coming-of-age ceremony. She looked in the hollow for a note but only found a little wooden box with a silver ribbon.

She opened the box and saw a little note on top of a silver moonstone ring.

She opened the note after slipping the ring onto her right ring finger.

My little witch,

You are my moon. Dance for me in the moonlight every time you wear this ring.

Your wolf,

Zaiden

"Damn it!" she called out, wishing it wasn't late.

She leaned against the tree as she heard a twig snap in the tree line of the woods. She smiled, hoping he had returned, even if it was in his wolf form.

"Zaiden?" she called, searching for him.

The menacing growl told her she was not alone, nor was it her wolf. The large black wolf lunged at her making her throw up her hands, casting a spell in defense. She was able to slow the wolf down, but it wouldn't be enough. She turned and began to run as the memory of Zaiden's warning echoed in her mind.

'Not all are as kind as I. Call for me if another wolf comes to you.'

She screamed, "ZAIDEN!" She sprinted through the long willow tendril branches hoping they would buy her moments where she could escape.

Her feet knew the graves well, but soon she felt the searing pain run down her back as the cool death-soaked earth captured her fall. Her head bounced off a stone hidden beneath a slight coating of the first leaves of fall. She felt the breath leave her lungs as her body ached from her sudden stop, but fear filled her again as she heard the growl.

Her body throbbed and longed to stay on the ground, but she began to slowly move, trying to get away from her hunter. The place she had grown to love was now her nightmare as it spun in agonizing pain.

She fell back against the ground as she rolled on her back, seeing the wolf with golden eyes come to stand over her, ready to introduce her to death.

She closed her eyes, and tears rolled down her temples. She let the happiest thoughts of her and Zaiden fill her mind, accepting her fate and that she would never see the man and wolf she had come to love again.

She heard a snarl and felt the wolf fall away from her. She opened her eyes slowly to see a large white wolf attacking the large black one. She watched the fight go on for what felt like an eternity as her eyes slowly closed against her will. Darkness enshrouded her as the smell of hot copper filled her senses.

Zaiden forced himself to transform back into his human state as he rushed over to her. He gently picked her up and carried her back into the shadows to the cobblestone house he had escorted her to many times before, but he never had walked up to the house or been inside. He knew he could be walking to his death, but he would do it if it meant it could save her.

He held her close to him as he kicked the door. "I mean you no harm. I have your daughter. She is hurt."

Soon the door opened, and he saw a silver-haired woman who could have been an older version of Maddie. She looked at his naked form and then at Maddie in shock before backing up to let him in.

"What happened to her? Are you a werewolf?!" The woman cried, clearing the table, so he could lay Maddie down on it.

"I am. She was attacked by another wolf…while she was waiting to see me," he admitted as he laid Maddie down as gently as possible. "She has claw marks on her back, and I believe she hit her head on a rock. I will step aside and let you work, but I won't leave her until *she* tells me to go," he warned the woman.

"She went to see a werewolf! She carries wolfsbane. I grow it all around our home to keep your kind away!" she yelled as she quickly gathered a bowl of clean water and rags to clean the wound on her head.

"It doesn't deter us! It was a lie my ancestors started to keep yours from killing our kind because they thought we were killing their children. It actually attracts us." He said, watching Maddie's chest rise and fall with each breath.

"What would you want with her anyway?" she asked, looking at his naked form.

"She bewitched me as a child. I can't explain what happened. It was the winter solstice moon, and she was playing with her kitten in the graveyard. I didn't think she could see me, but she did, and there was something…I don't understand the connections of witches! I have protected and befriended her since then…but since she came of age…." he stopped himself.

"What, wolf?" she asked him harshly.

"I stopped seeing her as a child I was protecting. Instead, I saw a beautiful young woman…I started to fall in love," he admitted, as he sat in a chair across from Maddie.

Her mother stopped and looked at him surprised, "You love her…."

"I have always loved her!" he yelled, then paused. "This love was different…"

"Your kind and mine both forbid it."

"I know it's forbidden. If I could stop loving her, I would! I can't…" he paused, knowing either death was coming or his time with her was ending. He looked at Maddie one last time, touched her leg, and fought back his own pain. "You don't have to cast me out. I will go." He stood, believing he knew his fate.

As he reached the door, she began to speak, "I wouldn't dare cast you out. Maddie's father was a werewolf. Witches are already supernatural beings, so that is why she never became one, but it could explain why she had a connection to you. He died, and I found out I was pregnant with her. That is when my mother told me that wolfsbane would keep wolves away. I wanted her to be far from your kind, but instead, she found you without trying. I…I can't bring her the pain I suffered when Draklin died. Stay." she said, looking up at him, "I am Analise. You may call me Ana." As he turned back to her, surprised. "Now, could you hand me the jars of willow's bark and frankincense resin? I will make a paste for her wounds. She has a concussion, but she should be all right," she told him with a gentle smile.

He walked to the shelf across the room, gathered the jars, and returned them to her.

"Sit here with her while I make the paste," Ana told him as she stood.

He sat down and moved the chair closer to her before softly running his fingers over her head. Her hair was still as silky and smooth as when he first touched it. He gently picked out the leaves her mother had missed. He wiped his eyes as he heard footsteps walking back toward the table and took a deep breath.

"Should I get out of your way?" He asked her as his voice broke a bit.

"No. I can feel her energy is stronger with you close to her. There was always a piece of her that was missing when she would return home from her adventures. I now can see that you were that piece. Your fate strings are entwined with each other. Help me roll her over, so I can take her dress off and treat those deep claw marks on her back," Ana said, starting to roll her over.

He gently helped roll her over as he watched Ana undo the black lace and cotton dress ruined by the rogue wolf's claws. As she began to pull the dress from Maddie, he looked away.

"You have never seen her…" she said, noticing him turn away.

"Not once. If she ever gave that part of herself to me, I

would be honored, but I have never even asked. I meant it when I said I protected her. All of her, including her dignity."

Ana smiled softly as she worked on her daughter, spreading the paste over her wounds and bandaging them. Then they gently rolled her back as they heard a groan from Maddie.

He quickly got a blanket from the back of an old rocking chair and handed it to Ana. "Cover her, please."

Ana nodded and wrapped her in the blanket. "Will you carry her to her bed? All she needs is rest and to let the herbs and healing magic work."

Zaiden nodded and gathered her up gently again before following Ana down through a darkened hallway into a bedroom. The scent of dried flowers filled his nose. He looked around, seeing dried bouquets of nightshade, roses, and lilies. His eyes then caught all the things her bedroom was filled with, the things he had made her, trinkets, and oddities they had found on their many walks.

He laid her on the bed and made sure she was well covered. He heard Ana slowly moving around the room.

"Since she turned fifteen, I gave her space and never came in here. Otherwise, I would have had many concerns about her collection." She picked up a small wooden carving of a crescent moon. "Did you make this for her?" she asked him as her memory was flooded with the things she kept hidden in a box from Draklin.

"I did. She was seventeen when I gave that to her. After full moon rituals, she would come to the old willow in the graveyard and wait for me. I gave her that before the midsummer moon. She was so happy…" he said, chuckling. "I can't even remember now why she was so happy, but she asked me to run with her in the moonlight and dance," he said, still smiling at the memory. "It was our ritual to run to the lake and swim in the warm waters on that moon after that night."

"That was the night of the first ritual she got to lead in our coven. She did it so well. The energy was so strong and wild. It was perfect." She set the trinket back down and smiled at him. "I feel like I have missed so much of her life, but I am sure my mother felt the same. Stay with her. I will be nearby if either of you needs me."

Zaiden was still surprised that he was welcomed into a witch's home, but now everything made sense to him. He transformed into the large white wolf, climbed up next to her, and laid against her. He closed his eyes, praying to the old Gods to speed her healing.

Hours felt like days as they passed slowly, but soon she drifted out of the darkness, and her senses returned to her body. She felt warm and safe as her eyes began to open. She reached up and touched her forehead and winced a bit. Her eyes began to focus as she saw she was home in her bed. She looked down seeing a large white wolf sleeping close to her.

She tried to speak, but her voice came out only in a whisper. "Zaiden?" A whisper was all that was needed.

Zaiden's eyes shot open as she saw her looking at him. He transformed back to his human form and softly caressed her face.

"You are alive! How are you feeling?" he asked her, his eyes never leaving hers.

"Alright. Did you bring me home? Where is my mother?"

she whispered.

"Your mother is pretty amazing. I was fairly sure she would murder me when I brought you here," he said softly.

"I am glad she didn't. I would have never forgiven her for killing you," she whispered.

"Let me get you some wat…" He was interrupted by a knock at the door. He jumped up and opened it, seeing Ana carrying breakfast for them both and some hot tea for Maddie. "A witch. I should have known." he said, chuckling.

"You will get used to it."

"I really should go get some clothes," he said softly.

"There are some that should fit you in the living room," Ana said to him sweetly as she handed Maddie a cup of tea.

Zaiden left them to have a moment together while he dressed. He wanted to be close to Maddie, but he knew there was a time for that later.

As he closed the door, Ana smiled, "So, you are in love with a werewolf? That is a dangerous path, but you couldn't help it if you wanted, could you?"

"No. Fate chose us. Are you angry? I know it is forbidden."

"Oh, hush now, little lass. Our family has never truly followed the rules. Fate has other plans for you. I only care about your safety and happiness. He can give you both."

Ana smiled as she heard the floorboards creak, "I think this will be the last we see each other for a while, isn't it?"

Maddie sat quietly for a moment, then spoke, "I think so. After last night I realized..."

Her mother pressed her fingers against her lips. "I know. I need to go gather some mushrooms. Be safe, my little wolf." With that, her mother got up and left the room. "Love her always, Zaiden," she told him as she walked past him.

Zaiden walked into the room, "Did I miss something?"

Maddie smiled, "She is a strong witch and can see the future. She knows I will be leaving with you."

He smiled and walked over to her, "Only if that is what you want. It is the only way I know to keep you safe."

"It is the only thing I desire," she said softly before leaning in and kissing his lips. "I have always loved you." She tilted her head and kissed him deeper this time.

A few short days later. Maddie left the cobblestone cottage for the last time holding Zaiden's hand. Zaiden carried a pack of her belongings on his back. They made their way to the graveyard and to the willow one last time as if they were there to say goodbye to the dead. When she was ready, she took his hand, and he led her into the woods' shadows and the world she would call home.

Little Bear

Honesty knows no bounds.
Strength unsurpassed.
Endless love.
Resilience within.
Carve your path,
Let nothing stop you.
You are strong.
You fight for what you love.
When all seems dark,
Remember, you are loved.
Rest now,
Winter has come.
The cave is safe,
You are home.

Flames of Fandom

Rylie

This was supposed to be the ultimate girls' weekend that I had been planning for months with my girlfriends, but now they have bailed on me—months of planning just gone in an instant. I suppose I could go alone, but who wants to go to New Orleans alone? I would look like a sad or desperate girl looking for hookups. No, I couldn't do that.

I flopped on the couch and groaned as the front door opened. A smile crept over my lips as I saw my roommate, Jeremy, walk through the door from work. Jeremy was the best roommate a girl could dream of and handsome, too. I would never admit that he had been featured in some of my fantasies, but I am a sucker for his dark hair and those hazel eyes. He turned and walked over and patted my knee as those eyes gave me a once over.

Jeremy and I had been friends for years and roommates for the last three. He was the best thing in my life. We were opposites to our cores, no matter how we tried to get each other to cross over into our dark sides. He was a nerdy gamer, and I was a goth bookworm.

"Shouldn't you be packing for your girl's getaway?" he asked with that smirk that I loved dearly.

I sighed, frustrated, "Nope. It got canceled. They bailed on me for something with Izzy's boyfriend."

He lifted my feet and placed them on his lap as he sat with me. "Well…I could have a solution since you are free and need some adventure."

"What? A gothic romantic trip for two to haunted Savannah?" Sass dripped from my words.

"Umm…no. I have an extra ticket to the Galaxy Fandom Convention this weekend. There is shopping, you could meet some of those dark and twisty cosplayers, and there are a few parties with dancing. Come with me? I promise it will be a good time." He sounded hopeful as his eyes met mine.

I knew he was going alone, but part of me didn't want him to be lonely. "Okay, fine. Help me pack since I have no idea what is needed?"

He stood laughing and helped me up. "All right, but if I'm helping you, I get to pick what I want."

I was suddenly wondering if I would live to regret this decision. I grabbed my small suitcase from the hall closet as he began to look through my closet. When I returned to the bedroom, he had picked out a pair of jeans and tee shirts, but then he took out my black dress—the one I only wear on dates.

"Not that," I said, reaching for the dress in his hands.

He quickly pulled away from my grasp. "Nope, I get to pick. That was our deal. Why don't you wear this dress very often?"

I felt my cheeks grow warm. "It's my date dress. I haven't been on a date in a while."

He nodded as there was a flash of something I couldn't read in his eyes. "Well, you will need something to wear to the parties. So, the dress is going."

I groaned. "Really? You want me all dolled up for a geek fest? I am going to be swarmed by guys in that dress."

His eyes met mine and darkened a bit. "Not if they know you are mine."

I had to look away because my deep blush felt like it had spread over my whole body. Jeremy and I had always flirted, but this level of confidence was new, and it brought out a new level of excitement within me.

"There you go. No changing the outfit selections either. Honor our deal," he said as he started out of my room to get his stuff.

I went and looked over the outfits. I was now wondering if this weekend was more as friends or if it was more of a romantic getaway. He must have known my romantic getaway comment was a joke, right? I quickly packed the clothes, sleepwear, and everything else I needed.

I walked out, almost running into him. I blushed, feeling his hands on my hips to steady me. His hands squeezed softly before letting me go. It was as if he was fighting an urge inside of him. *Had things changed between us, and I missed the signals?*

Jeremy

I swear the Gods were trying to torture me with this woman. *Don't fuck things up, Jeremy. You have to do this right if you want to win her and keep your best friend.* I pulled my hands from her hips, though the Gods knew I didn't want to. I gave her one of those smirks that always made her blush a little as I ran my fingers through my hair.

"You ready to go? We have about an hour's drive to the hotel." He started grabbing her bag from her hand. "Oh, I almost forgot we will have to share a room. They are sold out 'cause of the Con. I can crash on the floor if you are uncomfortable." I said as I headed out to the car with her.

"No, that is no problem. I would never let you sleep on a hard hotel floor. Just don't get too handsy in your sleep," she said.

I laughed, "I can make no promises about my subconscious, but I will try."

I handed her my phone and told her to pick some music while I drove.

"Your background is us? That's cute. I hope the girls you date don't mind," she said before opening my Spotify.

Shit. I force a laugh to try to play it off. "What girls? I work, play games, and hang out with you. There hasn't been a girl in my life for a while. Unless you count you."

She giggled. "I don't think hanging with your bestie counts as a date."

If she only knew how much I loved that photo of us. Her long raven hair parted on the side, her hazel green eyes, and soft full lips…fuck, she was perfect. That photo was my background because I wanted it to be my goal. I have been crazy about her for years, but I always told myself it was better to be friends than risk losing her forever. I don't know how much longer I can keep telling myself that.

I glanced over at her and felt contentment well up within me as I watched her softly sing the songs. I swear she caught me watching during one of my glances and blushed. Gods, she was perfect.

The drive was easy. We laughed and flirted. I could have sworn she tried to hold my hand at one point, but it was as if she caught herself and pulled back. This weekend would prove one of two things. She wanted to be mine, or I was going to lose her. The very thought of that made my heart want to shatter.

Rylie

I felt myself slipping into our comfortable state, but there was something different this time. It felt more like that request for a romantic getaway. Each time we flirted, it felt more profound and less like the playfulness of our past flirtations. I dreamed of this, but I would never want to ruin our friendship.

My thoughts haunted me as we arrived at the hotel. After he checked us in, we headed up to our room. The large king bed reminded me I would be sharing a bed with him for the next three nights. I hung up my dress and fixed my makeup just in time for us to head down to the opening ceremonies.

He leaned against the door frame with his arms crossed, meeting my gaze in the bathroom mirror. "I don't think you could get more beautiful. Are you almost ready? We should go if we want to get good seats." There was a hunger in his eyes that I couldn't track. I wouldn't admit it out loud, but I liked it.

"Yep. I just wanted to get my lipstick just right in case I meet High Lord Viktor or something."

"Oh? You want a good rough choke from Viktor?" he said with a husky tone.

I blushed deeply. "He is pretty much the only one I know besides that cute squealing robot and Owen. Oh, and I think the one named Lyra." I grabbed my purse, slung it over my body, and walked out with him.

"I promise to keep you in the loop so you won't feel lost," he said as he pulled my hand around his arm.

Jeremy

I prayed that this weekend alone with her wasn't a mistake. Watching her put her lipstick on those perfect lips made my body crave her in a way I didn't realize was possible. I had fantasized about her so many nights, but now they were starting as so many had played out in my mind.

Soon, we were making our way through the crowd as I guided her to some seats as close to the stage as possible. After we sat, I gave her a taste of the Con experience. I pulled out my phone and pulled up the schedule for Saturday.

"Look through the events and tell me what you would like to see." It seems as if my body has a mind of its own as my arm slips around her shoulders.

I smiled, feeling her snuggle into my embrace. I loved how she always seemed to crave when I touched her. I watched her scroll through the list, slowly reading the descriptions. I know this wasn't her usual thing, but seeing her try was an amazing feeling, even if it was just for me.

"Anything catching your fancy, love?" I asked her softly.

"I am shooting in the dark, maybe the one with that guy in the armor who never takes it off…and maybe the one Owen one. I don't know, really. What do you want to see?" she asked, smiling.

"Oh, I would be happy to see several, but those sound good," I said, smiling as I took my phone and slipped it back into my pocket as the ceremony started.

The Master of Ceremonies highlighted several events and the after-parties. I felt her lean close to whisper to me, and as she did, her hand slipped over my thigh.

"Are we going to the party tonight?" she whispered in my ear.

I brushed her hair away from her ear as I leaned in and whispered close so she would feel my breath on her ear. "Yes, we are. Wear your dress for me."

Her grip on my thigh tightened slightly. "For you?" she replied.

"Yes, for me," I said, trying to hold back my desire and of longing to see her in that dangerous dress.

She turned and met my eyes as if searching for an answer to an unasked question before nodding.

Rylie

I still can't believe I agreed to wear this dress tonight. He seemed obsessed with me wearing it. I did look great, and when I entered the ballroom, I realized exactly how good I looked. I could feel eyes on me, but the only eyes I searched for were his. I found him chatting up a few folks across the room, and I wanted to reach his side. I don't know why I felt like a deer walking through a forest of wolves waiting for me to be their next meal. It wasn't long before a man approached me. His gruff appearance made me uneasy.

"Well, hello there," he said with a smile that made my stomach turn.

"Hi. Not trying to be rude, but I am late meeting someone," I said, trying to step away, but he cut me off.

"Oh, and who is that? They can't be as fun as I am."

I pointed to Jeremy, seeing him look over and then turn toward me. "Him."

"That guy? He doesn't look like he would be your type," he said, stepping closer to me.

I took a step back and looked at Jeremy, who was making his way over to me.

"We are… he is my type." My words were shakier than I expected.

Before the creep could answer, I felt lips on mine. I was surprised to feel Jeremy's lips.

He broke the kiss. "Hey, beautiful. Ready to dance?"

I nodded as he took my hand and started to lead me away without a word to the man. I was still trying to wrap my head around the situation as I felt Jeremy pull me close as we swayed to the music.

"You kissed me…" I stammered out.

"Yes. It was either that or try to break that guy's face, but that would have gotten us kicked out of the hotel and Con. I could see you were uncomfortable, and I wanted to make you feel safe again," he said, holding me tighter.

"How did you know I wouldn't have hit you?" I asked, feeling myself start to relax in his arms. He always knew exactly how to calm my nerves.

"Well, it was a risk I was willing to take," he smirked.

I was quiet for a moment. "Well, it was a good kiss."

I felt him move my hair away from my neck. "No, it wasn't."

I pulled back a bit to meet his eyes. "Yeah, it was. I was there."

He chuckled. "Rylie, if I were to kiss you for real, you would be quivering when I finished. You would feel it here..." he said as his finger touched between my breasts and then slipped down. "And here..." As it rested on my belly. "Finally, you would be a dripping mess when I finished." He slipped his hand back around my waist.

"You are confident. You really think you could make me feel that from a kiss?"

"I know I could. Just because you haven't had it happen to you before doesn't mean I can't do it."

I was a bit insulted by him saying that. "How do you know it's never happened?"

"In all the years I have known you, you have dated a few guys, and you always would bitch to me about how they left you...unsatisfied." His hand seemed to rub the small of my back while we danced closer than we ever had.

"Fine, prove it if you are so confident you could do this. Kiss me like that and see if you are as successful as you think you are." I said, wondering if he was right, and Gods, I wanted to feel his lips just once more.

"What do I get if I am right?" He licked his lips as he looked into my eyes.

The song ended, and I pulled him into one of the darkest corners of the ballroom to finish this conversation. I didn't want the other wolves to see if he could make me melt like he claimed.

"What do you want besides bragging rights?"

I watched his eyes drift over me for a moment. "I want you to cosplay for the party with me tomorrow night."

"I don't have anything to cosplay as, remember? You packed my bag."

"You can buy cosplay costumes here. Get whatever you like."

"Fine, but what if you are wrong? What do I get?"

He smirked. "Besides bragging rights? What do you want?"

"Dinner at Rivera," I said with a sassy smile.

"At Rivera! The five-star restaurant? I feel like I am getting the short end of the deal." He sighed. "Fine."

"If you are as good as you say you are, you have nothing to worry about. So, we have a deal?"

He nodded and pulled me flush against him, making me gasp. His lips claimed mine like fire claims oxygen. His hand slipped up around my throat as his tongue slipped over mine. My hands slipped up his chest, grabbing the lapels of his suit jacket. Seconds felt like hours as his hands roamed my body. A moan escaped my lips as he grabbed my ass, pulling me into him. Soon, he began to pull away, and my lips searched for his, unwilling to let go. He smiled and tucked a piece of hair behind my ear.

I stood there panting softly and holding on to him as if my knees would give out if I let him go. My eyes met his. I hated that he was right, but Gods almighty, he was right. I was now in such a state of hunger and desire, and only he would satisfy.

"I…need a drink…" I said softly as I started to walk away before I let him fuck me right there.

I felt a hand grasp my wrist. I looked down to see him

holding on to me. He pulled me back to him and kissed me again, softer this time.

"You won…so what was that?" I asked, still fighting my arousal.

"I know. You needed it."

Jeremy

I let go of her and watched her walk to the bar, still reeling from that kiss. I felt her kiss me back, and her body's response to mine was perfection. The seed was planted, but now it would be a matter of time to see if it would grow over the next few days. I reached down and adjusted my pants to hide my own arousal before walking over to the bar to join her.

I ran my hand over the small of her back as she sipped what I could only guess was a whiskey. "You okay? I didn't break you, did I?"

She turned to me. "No…well, a little. It was just a bet, right?" she asked me with a tone in her voice that I couldn't read.

"Are you asking if I intended that to be more than just a bet, as you say? That depends on you. If you just wanted it to be a bet, that's what it was, but if not, I would be happy to pursue more. I know, I don't want to risk losing you." I admit, as I also order a whiskey.

"Lose me? Jeremy…I am not going anywhere. You are stuck with me. You would only lose me if you walked away." She took my hand and squeezed it softly. "What if I did want more?" she continued.

I watched the bartender place my drink in front of me before taking a sip. "If that is what you want, then I will give everything to make you my world, but if you don't, then don't tell me. I don't want to know if you don't." I take another sip of my drink. "Just think about it," I said, realizing this conversation moved up my timeline, but I couldn't lie to her.

I finished my drink before turning to her. "Still up for some more dancing?" I asked with a warm smile.

She nodded and took my hand as we returned to the dance floor. I pulled her back against me as we danced like she was mine and always had been.

Rylie

My head was swimming. Jeremy wanted more than our friendship. I wanted it too, but Gods, what if I lost him? He had been my best friend for nearly a decade, and now I had a choice to make.

As the music slowed, I felt him pull me tighter against him. I rested my head against his cheek as we swayed without words. It felt like time had stopped, but my focus was broken when I felt a tap on my shoulder. I looked as another man asked to cut in and dance with me. I don't know why, but my hand grasped Jeremy's tighter. When I looked up at Jeremy, the look in his eyes was almost a threat.

"No. She is mine," he replied calmly.

I blushed as the man grumbled and walked away.

"You know I am not yours…yet." I turned his gaze back to mine.

"I know. But he didn't. I know you aren't mine *yet*, but I

also don't want to see another guy's hands on you. Especially not in that dress." He said as he licked his lips like he was starving.

I rested my forehead against his chest. "Can we go back to the room? Please? I am overwhelmed." I said, needing to be away from the music and prying eyes. Most of all, I needed to talk to him.

Jeremy

I heard her pleas and nodded. *Did I fuck up already?* I guided her out of the ballroom to the elevator. I looked over at her and saw the conflict of emotions coursing through her. *Fuck.*

We reached the room in silence. As soon as I turned the lights on, she grabbed her pajamas and headed to the bathroom without a word. I took my blazer off, laid it over the chair back, and sat on the bed.

Fuck, fuck, fuck. My head rested in my hands as I heard the bathroom door open. I looked up and saw her dressed in yoga pants and a tank top.

"Rylie, I'm s-" I began before she cut me off.

"Jeremy… how long have you felt like this about me?" she asked as she came and sat on her side of the bed.

I was terrified to look at her. It felt like I had pushed too hard, too fast. "Years."

She was silent for what seemed like an eternity.

"Rylie, please say something… You are scaring me." My heart pounded in my chest.

"I can't lose you… I fuck up relationships. Gods, you know this! What if I fuck it up with you?" Her voice broke.

Fucking damn it! I vowed never to make her cry again. I was an ass and ripped our friendship apart one time four years ago. The pain I caused her, I swore I would never make her cry like that again. I could hear it in her voice, that same pain. The memory flooded back in my mind like a stab to the gut.

I had lost so much, and Rylie only wanted to save me from my pain. My job. My relationship with a woman who I thought loved me. I started to push Rylie away. She wasn't blind to my distance, and she called me on it. I told her I didn't fucking need her or want her. I will never forget watching the look on her face when I broke her heart. Some say you can't break a friend's heart, but I did. I ripped it from her chest.

She took me at my word. I watch tears flow down her cheeks. I took out my pain on the one woman who had only ever given me love. I regretted it immediately, but I had already fired that figurative shot.

It took months and even years to regain her complete love and trust. Now, I could hear that fear welling up in her voice.

"I am not going anywhere. Not now, not ever," I said, meeting her eyes.

"Even if I say no?" she said, trying so hard not to cry.

I wanted to pull her into my arms, but I might make it

worse if I did.

"You said the only way I would lose you is if I walked away…You would only lose me if you walked away from me. You are stuck with me, beautiful," I said with a soft smile.

Before I could react, she tackled me into a tight hug, almost knocking me off the bed. She held me tightly for a long time as if she were afraid I would disappear.

"I just can't lose you…not again." She said against my neck.

I swear my heart broke hearing her say that…'again.' Even if she told me fuck no to being mine, I would never intentionally hurt her again.

"You won't." I kissed the top of her head. After a long while, I felt her relax in my arms as her anxiety faded. "Come on, love. Let's get some sleep. We have a big day tomorrow. Nothing has to be decided tonight." I felt her nod and gave me a soft nuzzle before she returned to her side of the bed.

I undressed down to my boxers before crawling in bed with her.

"Tha-that's how you are going to sleep?" she said, watching me like I had committed a war crime.

"Uh…yes? I usually sleep naked, but I figured you would be uncomfortable with that." I said, looking at her as she crawled under the covers and rolled to face me.

"I just didn't know you slept naked. Did you always?"

I blushed a bit. "Yes, except on stormy nights or days when you had a rough day. You always seem to join me for a cuddle on those nights."

"You plan for nights I may end up in your bed for a cuddle? That's sweet and impressive," she said as she laid her hand on my arm, as her eyes began to close. "How did I not know you slept in the nude?" She asked curiously, but her tiredness could be heard in her voice.

"One, you never asked, and outside of me walking in on you in the shower by accident, we have never seen each other naked." I smiled at her touch and turned out the lights. *Maybe I didn't completely fuck things up.*

Rylie

The next morning, I woke up to an empty bed. I looked around the room and could hear the soft rushing of the shower. I took my phone from the bedside table and looked at the time. 7:38. The first event started at 8 a.m. I guess he doesn't want to go to that one.

I scrolled my phone momentarily before I heard a groan from the bathroom. I got up and headed closer to the door to listen and make sure he was okay. But then I heard another deeper groan…no, a moan. I listened to him with my ear close to the door.

"Fuuuckk, Rylie." Followed by a moan.

I knew how he felt, but listening to him fantasize about me and moan my name made me ache for him. Why couldn't I just tell him I needed to be his?

His moans got louder, and soon I heard him cum and moan my name again. How was I supposed to make it through today with those perfect moans echoing in my head? After a moment, I heard the shower turn off and rushed back to bed.

I heard the door open, and my breath caught in my throat. Fuck he was in a towel. A fucking towel!

"Ummm…good morning," I said softly as he almost jumped out of that towel.

"God damn, baby, I didn't realize you were awake." He said, then grimaced. "Sorry…the baby rolled out faster than I realized."

I couldn't help but blush. "It's okay. I like it."

His face lit up like a kid at Christmas who just got his first Xbox. "Well, I can keep calling you that if you want me to?"

I couldn't help but blush even more and nod. Damn it, Rylie, just say it! Say I want you too. Say I want to be yours, Jeremy!

"I…am starving. Let me shower, too, and then we can get breakfast." I mentally kicked myself for being a coward.

Heading for my suitcase, I picked out a pair of jeans and a tee shirt, then realized the shirt was his. "Did you pack the wrong shirt? This is yours."

"Wear it, babe. I am sure it will look great on you." He replied as he nudged me to the bathroom.

It wasn't unusual that occasionally his clothes would end up in mine, but he should have known it was his when he packed it. I closed the door behind me to the bathroom, still feeling the wet mugginess of the steam from his shower. I wanted nothing more than to call him into the bathroom to join me in the shower, but something in me stopped me. What am I so afraid of?

Turning the handle, I felt the soft rainfall of the water on my hand. I undressed and stepped under the cascade, hoping it would clear my head and give me more confidence. I needed him, and I think he knew what I was too afraid to say. I hope my anxiety won't destroy us.

Jeremy

As I dressed, I could hear the shower and soon wondered if she could also hear me. I prayed she didn't, even though I would give anything to feel her soft, naked curves under my hands. My mind was still reeling from her, allowing me to call her baby and feeling her wrapped in my arms all night. I felt like I was one step closer to making her mine. Today, we would find out how far I had pushed and if I could continue my pursuit.

It wasn't long until I heard the shower turn off. I hoped for a glimpse of her in a towel, but at the same time, I wanted to respect her space. *Why was I so nervous?* I hadn't been this tense when I kissed her, but now…I was practically shaking. I nearly jumped out of my skin when I heard the bathroom door open. *How long was I lost in my thoughts of her?*

"Good shower?" I asked, seeing she was dressed and drying her hair.

"Yeah, it was nice. A little lonely but nice." She said with a flirty smile. I let out a soft groan. This distance was killing me, but I knew it was necessary.

"Lonely, huh? Next time, just ask, and I will ensure you aren't alone." I replied, praying my nervousness wasn't showing.

She blushed and turned back to the bathroom.

Before I realized it, I was right behind her, pinning her against the counter. Spinning her around, I looked into her eyes and then down to her lips. I wanted to take her right there.

"Rylie…"

Rylie

I gasped, feeling him spin me to face him and pressing me between the counter and him. The hunger in his eyes excited me and also made me nervous. When I heard him say my name, it was more of a plea than a statement, and I couldn't help it. My arms wrapped around him and buried my face against his neck.

"It's not a yes yet…but just don't let go yet," I said against his neck.

He pulled me tight against him. "Baby, I won't let you go as long as you let me hold you. I won't ever let go. I need…I just needed to feel you against me." His tone was full of desire.

"Jeremy, I… am still making sure, but please, just one kiss?" I begged. I wanted so much more, but my fear of losing him was fighting my desire to be his.

His fingers slipped up and grasped my hair in the back gently, making me look at him. He looked into my eyes almost for confirmation of consent before his lips crashed into mine. The kiss was hotter than the first real one we shared. It was like a fire trying to be contained so it wouldn't consume us both. But I burned for him. I knew that now.

His free hand roamed my body, grasping and groping in the most perfect way as our tongues danced. A moan escaped my lips into the kiss as his fingers brushed against my breast.

He broke the kiss and growled. "I need to stop, or we will never leave this room. I need a yes to being mine before I go down that road. Take all the time you need, baby, but please, please…don't take too long." He said as he tenderly kissed my forehead and left me to finish getting ready.

I heard his words, but they took a moment to process before I could even move. I knew now I had to be his, but I wanted to make it more memorable. I wanted to show him I was ready to be his world.

Jeremy

Fucking hell, that woman would be the death of me! I loved her more than a flame loves oxygen. It took every fiber of my being to keep from walking back in there to her and taking her back to the bed. Seeing her dressed in my shirt and seeing it hugging her curves was going to drive me crazy. *What was I going to do if she said no? Would she say no after begging for that kiss? Gods, her begging might just be my kryptonite.*

I ran my fingers through my hair while I tried to let my desires calm down. I wanted her, but I knew until she said yes, I wouldn't take it any further. I hated it, but I think I had hit the line. I would have to wait for her to come to me now.

"Handsome? You ready to go?" she said, pulling me from my thoughts.

Hearing her call me handsome was like a siren's call. I knew at that moment by the end of this weekend, I wanted to risk it all just for her. She was my all.

I turned back to her and nodded. "Yeah, I am, baby. Are you?"

She smiled and held her hand out to me. "Let's go get geeky."

I laughed as I grabbed our lanyards. I put hers around her neck and moved her braid. I then put mine around my neck before taking her hand and leading her out of the room.

Rylie

The convention's main floor was bustling, full of convention goers and cosplayers. I held Jeremy's hand tightly as he led me through the crowd. Tables and vendors lined the hallways outside the ballrooms and dozens of people crowded around the various vendors. We wandered through the crowds until we reached one of the ballrooms where our first panel would be.

Jeremy made sure we got seats as close to the stage as possible. As we sat down, his arm slipped around me.

"Jeremy?" I said softly as my eyes met his.

"Yes, love?" he replied with a soft smile.

"May I ask for a favor?" I couldn't help but feel like I was asking for the crown of his kingdom.

"I will do anything for you, babe."

I smiled, meeting his eyes. "Would you mind if we separated for a bit after this panel?"

Concern filled his eyes, "We can, but why?"

My voice lowered as the panel began. "A surprise. If I told you, I might have to kill you."

He growled softly in my ear. "Okay, babe. Just be careful."

Jeremy

I held her close during the panel, hoping my touch would be soothing for her. I could sense her anxiety. Her touch and smile were like oxygen, feeding the flames of desire in me. The panel should have been something I was thrilled to listen to, but I couldn't stop thinking about her. After everything from last night and this morning, being separated from her felt like a horrible idea. I am usually not the type of guy who is possessive, but there was a feeling I couldn't shake. If this were the fandom, it would be a disturbance. *Would she trust me if I told her how I was feeling?*

Time slipped away, and before I realized it, the panel was ending, and everyone was applauding, drawing me from my thoughts. I pulled my arm from her and applauded before standing up. I took her hand and led her back out into the large hallway.

"So, where should we meet when you finish this secret mission of yours?" I asked her, still holding her hand. *Gods, what had me so nervous about letting her go?*

She giggled. "How about I text you, and we can meet back by the elevator?" she said as she looked up into my eyes.

I nodded. "I will make sure my phone is on extra loud so I will hear it. Be careful, babe." I said before kissing her cheek.

She looked at me concerned. "That is twice you have told me to be careful. Is there something I should be worried about?"

I smiled. "No, I guess I am just a little protective after that guy last night."

She smiled and kissed my lips quickly before leaving my grasp. I hoped that meant she was just about to be mine.

Rylie

I hoped that kiss soothed his worries, but his concerns seemed more than he was letting on. I made my way through the crowd to the vendor's space. I was overwhelmed at first, but after a few minutes, I found a vendor who sold cosplay costumes. There were so many choices and so many fandoms. I looked through what felt like dozens until I finally found one. It wasn't a traditional one, and it was more along the sexy Halloween side, but it was exactly what I wanted.

After purchasing it, I made my way around, looking at all the geeky knickknacks and fandom memorabilia. I couldn't help but buy a few things for him and myself.

I made my way back to the elevator and headed up to our room to drop things off. After dropping everything off, I took out my phone and texted him.

"Hey, handsome. I am heading to the elevator." I hit send and went down to meet him.

Jeremy

I felt my phone buzz and my notification sound go off loudly. I pulled it out quickly and smiled as I saw her message. I wasted no time heading to my girl. When I saw her by the elevator, I made my way to her through the large crowd. Seeing her face light up when she saw me made me feel like the luckiest man alive.

She threw her arms around me and smiled. "Miss me?"

I laughed and kissed her lips softly. "I did. Ready to go grab some lunch?"

She blushed and nodded as she took my hand. I led her outside across the street to the line of food trucks waiting to feed the masses for the Con. After a few minutes, we finally decided on tacos and got in line. After getting our food, we found a nice spot to sit and eat.

Rylie

We both were quiet for most of our meal. We were happy to enjoy each other's company, but something was weighing on me, and I knew we had to talk about it before we could take any more steps toward a future together.

"Jeremy…before we take any more steps, I need you to understand my hesitation," I said as he finished his last bite.

He turned to me, showing me I had his full attention, but I could see the worry on his face.

I took a deep breath. "That night. The one where we had that huge fight. The things you said…"

He cut me off. "Rylie, I have wished I could take back that night a million times over. I regret it…" I put my finger to his lips.

"Please let me finish. It hurts more than I like to admit talking about it." I looked down at my hands as I pulled my fingers back to fidget with my rings. "I was in love with you. I didn't realize it until you told me you didn't need or want me." My hands balled into fists, digging my nails into my palms, fighting back my tears. "I know it is not the same, but it was like you told me you didn't love me. I lost a man I loved and my best friend all at the same moment. I know now you never meant to hurt me… I know that anger and those words were not truly directed at me. I know that rationally now. But the pain is still there. You broke my heart. It never really healed. I am so scared to feel that again… I love you. Gods almighty… I love you, Jeremy. I am so terrified to let myself be yours. What if…you do it again? I won't make it a second time." I concluded, not realizing my tears had fallen and were rolling down my cheeks.

When I looked up at him, the look on his face was like I had gutted him and killed his puppy simultaneously. *What did I do?*

He sat there stunned for what felt like an eternity. "Jeremy… Please say something."

He leaned forward and brushed my tears from my cheeks. "I hate myself for even thinking of causing you pain. But I have to live with that. I know I have promised you I would never hurt you again, but we are human. We will both hurt each other, but we have to promise to work through it. I didn't. I hurt you and left you in that pain. My own pain blinded me to what I did to the only woman who truly loved me. I understand your hesitation. I just hope you will let me love you like you deserve. You deserve the world, baby."

I hated that this pain was shared between us, but now he understood my fears. I kissed him softly. I couldn't help it. "I promise I won't make you wait much longer. You will know my decision by tonight."

He smiled and pulled me close, holding me as my anxiety started to ease.

Jeremy

I felt like a monster. I knew I had broken her heart, but to hear how deep the wound I had caused was gut-wrenching. I couldn't undo it, but if she would let me, I would spend my life making sure I never hurt her like that again, and if I could, I would save her from any other pain. She had been through enough in her life and deserved love and peace.

"I will wait impatiently. Only because I long to call you mine. I love you too." I replied, realizing now my own tears stung my eyes.

I closed my eyes tight, fighting to keep them in. For the next few hours, my life would sit in her perfect hands until she made her decision. I prayed to every god in existence in that moment that my past wouldn't fuck up my future.

"We got time for a few more panels before tonight, or if you would rather rest or hang out, that would be fine too. I want to make sure you are having a good time. I also don't want to rush any decisions." I told her, still not quite letting her go.

She nuzzled my neck and nodded before she slowly pulled back. "Yeah, let me just get a little cleaned up, then we can continue on. I will need a good hour or two to get ready for tonight, and you can't see until the party," she said as she wiped her tears.

"Like, at all?"

"Nope, I want it to be a surprise. Promise no peeking?" she said, holding out her pinky.

"I promise. But I will miss you," I said playfully, pouting as I took her pinky and made the promise.

She blushed and giggled. "It will be totally worth it," she said before heading to the bathroom to clean up from her tears and smudged makeup.

I watched her go as I let my mind wander to what she had planned for tonight. She seemed excited to keep up her end of the bet from our first kiss. As much as I wanted to see what she had planned, I would have been just as excited to see her in those black yoga pants and the hoodie she loves. Every time she wore it, all I wanted to do was take it off of her and worship her like the goddess she is.

I jumped slightly when I felt a hand touch my shoulder. I turned and saw her, and I couldn't help but smile like a lovestruck fool. I took her hand and led her through the crowd to a panel. We held hands the whole time, and I felt like I couldn't breathe, not knowing her answer.

When the panel finished, I checked the time. "Why don't I go grab us a pizza for dinner, and you can start your beauty transformation? I won't look, we can just have dinner. Then I will get dressed and head downstairs."

She smiled. "Okay, handsome. I will meet you in our room."

Rylie

I hated making him wait, but I wanted this to go off perfectly. He deserved to see how invested I was for him. I went to our room and decided to start getting ready while waiting for him to return.

When I headed to the bathroom, I started the shower and quickly undressed. I needed just a moment to clear my mind before he returned. I craved his touch. I craved his lips. Most of all, I yearned to be his. Now that he knew my pain was viscerally deep, I knew he understood why I was so scared to let him love me. I needed him to love me. Jeremy was everything I needed. I just never thought until this weekend that he would want me. I had been so wrong for maybe years. *Is this why he always tried to get me to break up with every guy I dated?* The truth was he was right. They all left me unsatisfied, and at the end of every date, I wanted to run back to him.

I finished my shower and dried off before slipping into one of the fluffy bathrobes the hotel provided. I took out the cosplay dress and hung it in the steamy bathroom to remove any wrinkles. I closed the bathroom door so he wouldn't chance seeing it. I went and sat on the bed, crossed-legged, and scrolled on my phone. Not long after I sat on the bed, I heard the door open.

"Pizza's….here…" He said as he came around the corner and saw me. "Baby… I..fuck…" He looked me over and almost dropped the pizzas he was carrying.

I blushed deeply and giggled as I started to help him.

"No, stay! Please? If you come too close, I may take that robe off you. God damn." He said as he took a shaky breath.

"It's just me in a robe. Not lingerie." I say, giggling.

"It might as well be. I am presuming you are naked under that fluffy thing?" He said, setting the pizzas on the bed.

I nod, still giggling. I really liked seeing him so flustered.

He took a deep, slow breath. "You are a fucking tease. I would much rather dine on you, but I promised to behave until you said you were mine." He growled.

"I can go change… Oh, but do me a favor! Close your eyes. Please?"

"Okay…why? Also, don't you dare change!"

I quickly got up and shushed him. "Just close those sexy eyes and keep them closed until I say so, and no peeking!" I said as I watched him close his eyes.

I rushed to take the dress out of the bathroom and hid it in the closet and then grabbed out 'his and hers' matching bracelets. I stood in front of him and took his hand. I ran my thumb over his palm lovingly before I placed the small box on his palm. I giggled and kissed his cheek softly. I felt his other hand grab the belt of the robe.

"Babe…you are playing a dangerous game. I will beg if I must…" He growled.

I giggled. "Open your eyes, and no, you don't get to see me naked. Not yet, at least." I said as I pulled his hand off the belt and tightened it so he couldn't see anything.

He took another deep breath before looking down at the box. "What's this? Can I open it?"

I nodded. "Of course. I got one for you and one for me, but you don't get to see mine until tonight."

He opened the box and pulled out the leather bracelet with the silver ornately engraved charm that read 'Her Prince.' He looked at it and pulled me to him as his lips pressed against mine.

After a moment, he let me go. "I am sorry, babe. I love it so much, and that kiss was the only thing I could think of doing to say thank you."

I couldn't help but blush and giggle happily. "You are welcome, handsome."

He hugged me once more before nuzzling my neck. "I am going to grab a slice and then get ready. I want to be near you so badly, but you are driving me insane in the best of ways in that robe." He growled in my ear before stepping back.

I let out a soft sigh and nodded. I didn't want him to let go, but I understood how he felt. I was feeling it, too. I was not about to ruin my plans by giving in to my desires.

Jeremy

I couldn't believe how stunning she was in just a robe. I

was about to lose my composure. I needed her like air. I quickly ate two slices of pizza as I took out my cosplay of Sir Rikkard, my favorite knight from my favorite game.

I loved cosplaying, but I couldn't wait to see her cosplay. I know she had a plan for tonight, but the suspense of tonight was driving me wild. As I finished grabbing my key and wallet, I smiled at her, silently praying the Gods would allow her to be mine.

"Alright, baby, you have the room all to yourself. I will see you downstairs. Please don't take too long."

"I won't. Now, off you go!" she told me while she shooed me out the door.

I headed out the door and instantly missed her. I hope she won't take long to be by my side again.

Rylie

I was finally ready. I couldn't wait to see his reaction. This dress made me feel so sexy and slutty at the same time. I only prayed that I would get to him before another creep could see me and stop me.

I walked down the hall to the ballroom, and so many people complimented me on the dress. I walked into the ballroom and made my way through the crowd to him at the bar. I took a deep breath and tapped him on the shoulder.

"Hi, babe. So how do I look?"

Jeremy

The moment I laid my eyes on my girl, I lost the ability to process words. I stand corrected. She looked perfect in a robe, but this dress was even better.

The soft straps of silk covered her full breasts before slipping around her waist. Sheer-flowing fabric covered her legs, and the slits up to the hips were enough to make my mouth water. She was Rikkard's sorceress. Her long raven hair was down in soft curls, and she looked like a seductive demoness ready to claim my soul, and I would let her.

She stepped forward, took my hand, and led me to the dance floor. My mouth still gaped at how beautiful she looked. She stepped up into my arms and pressed her lips to my ear. She kissed my ear lobe and neck softly as we began to sway to the music. I desperately needed to hear if she was going to be mine. I needed to hear those words.

"Rylie, please…" I said as my hand buried in her hair.

"Jeremy, I promised you a night of dancing and fun… but from the look upon your face and hearing your desires earlier…I need you. I give myself to you. I am yours, now and forever. Claim me as you have been craving," she whispered before she pressed her lips to mine, kissing me softly.

I grasped her hair and pulled her tightly against my body as my lips claimed hers. She was finally mine. The Gods have answered my pleas and given me a woman I did not deserve, but she was MINE. I growled, breaking the kiss before looking her over once more.

"I will enjoy that dress another time, but we are missing this party. Upstairs. Now." I commanded as I led her to the elevator. The question was, would I make it to our room before I would make her cry out in pleasure?

Once the elevator doors closed, I pinned her against the

wall and kissed her with all the fire that had been consuming me for the last couple of days. My hand slipped down, grabbing her thigh and wrapping it around as we kissed ferally. I needed to feel her, but my own cosplay was keeping me from feeling my girl. I heard the elevator ding as I turned to see our floor. I was never more thankful and disappointed at the same time.

She pulled me to our room as I quickly got out the key and unlocked the door. As soon as the door was closed, she pressed me against the door, kissing me as she unleashed her desires.

My hands and hers quickly began to undo my cosplay armor from my body. As much as I loved my cosplay creation, at this moment, it was keeping me from feeling my sweet temptress's hands on my body. It wasn't long until we had done quick work, dropping all the pieces to the floor. She pulled my pants down and then dropped to her knees.

"Oh, my love…" I looked down at her, seeing her look up at me before her hand slipped around my rock-hard cock. I nodded, giving her the consent she needed.

Her tongue trailed up from my balls to the head of my cock before running around the head.

I let out a groan of pleasure as my breath caught. "Rylie, you have no idea how long I have wanted to feel your beautiful lips on my cock."

She smiled as her nails gently raked down my stomach, and her lips engulfed my member deep in her mouth.

I growled as I looked down and watched her slowly take as much of me as she could before releasing me. I didn't want to interrupt her beautiful worship, but I couldn't help my desire to claim her. My hands slipped over her head and buried in her hair.

"I am going to claim you as you requested. I may not be gentle. I may not be loving. But I promise I will give you so much pleasure you will see stars. Nod for me if this is what you want." I held her head firm, not letting her pleasure me until I had her consent.

She moaned as she nodded, pulled her hands from my body, and clasped them behind her back. She had given me her trust and submission. I thought I couldn't love her more, but here she was, making me love her more with each passing second.

I pulled my cock from her beautiful mouth before I leaned down and kissed her softly and lovingly. "I love you on your knees but do not want to ruin your dress. Take it off, and I will give you your next instructions, my sweet girl." I commanded.

Rylie

I was more than happy to get out of this dress for him. My body was on fire with desire for him. I needed his touch. I needed his domination. I needed him. I stood and slowly began to pull the fabric from my body, revealing my body to him like I was slowly unwrapping a gift for him. Watching the desire and hunger burn in his eyes was exhilarating. I was desperate for his praise and pleasure.

When the final piece of fabric fell from my body, I reached for my panties to slip them off and watched his hand fly up.

"Not yet. Put your dress away. Then, lay on the bed on

your back with your head just hanging off the edge. I am going to fuck that sassy and beautiful mouth." He said with a huskiness in his voice I had never heard before. It might be the sexiest thing I had ever heard.

I laid on my back on the bed and let my head hang off the bed as he instructed. I watched him walk over to me and softly caress my cheek.

"Pat your thigh three times if you want me to stop. Do you understand, kitten?" He said as he took his cock and ran it over my lips.

I nodded. "Yes…Sir." I said, testing the waters. In all the years I have known Jeremy, I had no idea how much of a dominant streak he had. I loved it so much.

He growled and smiled. "Good, kitten. Now open that mouth."

My mouth opened eagerly as he slipped his cock deep into my mouth and throat. I felt my eyes water, but I loved how he made me take it. A blush crept over my face as he started to fuck my mouth as if I had always been a good little slut for him. I couldn't help but moan as his perfect cock slipped in and out of my mouth. He leaned down, grasping my full breasts, and began to tease them as he used my mouth.

"Fuck, kitten! That's it. Take my cock." He groaned as his pace quickened.

Tears escaped my eyes, but I wouldn't ever want him to stop. I loved this as much as he did. I wanted to taste him. I wanted to hear his moans. Hearing him call me his kitten was everything I had dreamed of. It was like he knew exactly how to turn me into a perfect sub just for him. It was as if he was made to be mine.

Jeremy

Gods, her mouth was perfect. She was perfect. I looked down, watching her take my cock in her mouth as if she had done it a million times. She seemed to know exactly what I wanted. My pace quickened, and I knew it wouldn't be long until I flooded her sensuous mouth with my cum.

"Gods kitten... you are going to make me cum. I am going to give you this load deep down your throat. Are you going to be a good girl and take it?" I moaned, trying to keep my orgasm back long enough to see her response.

She moaned and arched her back like her body was begging for my cum. It was exactly the thing that sent me over the edge.

"Fucking Gods! Rylie!"

My hot cum began to spurt from my cock into her beautiful mouth. She never stopped sucking it from me as if she needed every drop.

I slowly pulled my cock from her mouth and leaned down and kissed her lovingly. "You are perfect and such a good girl for me. Fuck. Thank you, baby." I said between kisses.

She smiled. "That was so fucking hot. Also, don't call me 'baby' when I am naked. It's 'kitten' from now on," she said with that adorable giggle that made me know she would get her way with it.

"As you wish, my kitten. Now get up and take those panties off. I need you in my lap."

Rylie

I sat up and blushed as I saw him lying down on the bed. My own arousal was driving me to the point of sheer weakness for him. I would do just about anything he would ask of me. My body craved his touch. I quickly removed my panties at his command.

I straddled his lap feeling his cock press against my dripping folds. I let out a soft moan as I braced myself on his chest.

"Grind on me. I want to feel you drip with desire until you can't take it," he commanded.

I nodded and moaned as I started to slowly grind my pussy over his cock. Feeling him against me felt like a flame licking the air. His hands gripped my hips tightly as he let out a growl of pleasure.

"Just like that, Kitten. Fuck…" he said between moans.

His hands set the pace as I let him control my body. I didn't have the words to tell him how much I loved his domination of me.

"Sir… please…" I begged, desperate for him.

He growled and pulled me down on his cock, sinking deep into me. I let out a loud moan as he continued to guide my hips, making me ride him. My nails dipped into his chest as he set a slow and deep pace.

I needed so much more, but his grip on my body wouldn't let me change the pace.

"No, Kitten…be a good girl and follow my pace. I promise it will be worth it," he said, groaning in pleasure.

I pouted a bit, but I nodded. The slow pace was almost overstimulating, but I loved every second of it. His strong hands felt like they would leave bruises on my hips, but his dominating nature only turned me on more.

"Gods, I can feel you dripping. Do you need it badly? Tell me, Rylie. Tell me what you want," he said, meeting my eyes.

I panted. "I need it hard…please? I need you to fuck me and make me scream for you. I need…I want you…fuck…fuck me like you want to breed me…please?" My head was dizzy with lust. I wanted that book boyfriend fuck, and he was willing to give it to me.

He growled and rolled me on my back. "Fuck…You want that?" His hand slipped up my body until he wrapped his hand around my throat, thrusting deep into me.

I nodded as a loud moan escaped my lips. "Yes! Please?" I continued to beg as my hand roamed over his hand on my throat lovingly.

He leaned down and groaned in my ear. "Gods, you are perfect. Now take my fucking cock!" he said as his cock began to pound deep into my dripping pussy.

Jeremy

Watching Rylie moan for me and submit to me was the most beautiful thing I had ever seen. Her back arched as I thrust hard into her. She pulled my hand tighter around her throat as she gave me a sinful smile. I squeezed tighter as I felt her tighten around me.

I wanted to feel her explode on my cock. I needed it. She was my seductress, but I was the divine god she longed to worship.

I didn't stop my relentless primal thrusts as she pushed me closer to the edge. I wanted to flood her exquisite cunt with my cum. I wanted to make her scream in ecstasy.

Her nails raked down my chest, making me growl in

pleasure. "Fuck yes, Kitten! I am going to breed you! Fuck!"

Her body began to shudder as I released her throat. She began to cum hard, screaming in pleasure for me.

Feeling her tightening around me was everything I needed to tip over the edge. I moaned loudly as I thrust deep into her spilling my hot cum deep in her cunt. It was perfection. She was perfect.

I moved and laid next to her holding her close in my arms. "Rylie…I love you."

She heard my declaration as she turned and kissed me softly. "I love you too, Jeremy."

I softly caressed her face gently. "Now, here is to forever."

It had been six months since I won my girl over at that fandom convention. Life had been everything I had dreamed of, but now I knew I couldn't fight back on one last desire for her.

"Hey, you just about ready? I don't want us to miss our reservations," she said as I slipped on my suit jacket.

"Yeah, babe. Don't worry. We won't miss our special night at Rivera." I said as I slipped the small velvet ring box in my pocket.

May our flames burn forever.

About the Author

Brittany L. Adkins is a romance author who enjoys dipping her toes into all the subgenres of romantic fiction, including fantasy, horror, paranormal, contemporary, and erotic romance. Though she has an associate degree in Massage Therapy, she decided to follow her passion for writing to get her bachelor's degree in creative writing and fiction in 2016. She has always been an observer of people and culture, which has benefited her writing skills by allowing her to access knowledge of various cultures for depth in her characters and stories. This skill has always aided her in telling stories from multiple perspectives.

Many of her fellow writers have called her the Romantic Adventure Storyteller. She has also been mentored and created networking with writers in the entertainment and writing industry and the world of fandoms. She hopes her books will inspire an epidemic of reading.

Brittany, a podcaster, hosts two podcasts, Pagan's Witchy Corner and Pagan's Reading Nook. Both shows are available on your favorite podcast player. She is also a part-time blogger on Witchy Corner Productions. On her blog you can find book reviews, articles about homesteading and paganism and information on her books. She is also a landscape artist. Her art can also be found and purchased on her website.

Brittany lives in Tennessee on a small homestead with her husband, two children, and their dogs. She is also an MS warrior and enjoys reading, playing video games, and cosplaying in her free time.

Connect with her on social media.

Tiktok: @witchycornerproductions
Instagram: @witchycornerproductions
Website: www.witchycornerproductions.com

www.ingramcontent.com/pod-product-compliance
Lightning Source LLC
Chambersburg PA
CBHW020640180626
46816CB00003B/1059

9781732145337